Orient BlackSwan Abridged Texts

FAR FROM THE MADDING CROWD

Thomas Hardy

Abridged by
Manju Sambhunath Sen

Edited by
Seetha Srinivasan

Orient BlackSwan

ACKNOWLEDGEMENTS

The publishers and the editors would like to acknowledge thanks to Ralph W. V. Elliott and the Authors' Licensing and Collecting Society Ltd (ALCS), London for 'Narrative Technique' from *Far from the Madding Crowd,* London: Macmillan, 1966 and also to Thompson Publishing for a part of the chapter on 'Far from the Madding Crowd' from *The Complete Critical Guide to Thomas Hardy,* New York: Routledge, 2003. Though we have been in correspondence, permission has not been received at the time of going to press. But the publishers and the editors will furnish complete acknowledgement in future editions of this book.

ORIENT BLACKSWAN PRIVATE LIMITED

Registered Office
3-6-752 Himayatnagar, Hyderabad 500 029 (A.P.), India
E-mail: centraloffice@orientblackswan.com

Other Offices
Bangalore, Bhopal, Bhubaneshwar, Chandigarh, Chennai,
Ernakulam, Guwahati, Hyderabad, Jaipur, Kolkata,
Lucknow, Mumbai, New Delhi, Noida, Patna

First Published 2010

ISBN 978 81 250 3956 3

Typeset in Warnock Pro 10.5/12.5 by
OSDATA, Hyderabad 500 029

Printed at
Graphica Printers
Hyderabad 500 013

Published by
Orient Blackswan Private Limited
3-6-752 Himayatnagar, Hyderabad 500 029 (A.P.), India
E-mail: hyderabad@orientblackswan.com

Contents

Introduction

Life of Thomas Hardy

Thomas Hardy was born in the village of Higher Bockhampton in Dorset on 2nd June, 1840, in the early part of Queen Victoria's reign. His forefathers had lived there for many generations. He grew up surrounded by the rural aspects of life, soaking himself in the beauty of nature and absorbing the folklore, culture, and superstition of the countryside. Dorset became the Casterbridge of his novels. His tremendous love for the countryside and his impressions of country life and the people form the basis of many of his works. *Far from the Madding Crowd* is 'set in that region of the English countryside bounded by the river Thames in the north, the English Channel in the south, the Cornish coast in the west and in the east by a line running from Hayling Island to Windsor forest.' To this province Hardy gave the name Wessex and it formed the setting for several of his novels which were therefore known as the 'Wessex novels.'

Hardy's parents were inheritors of a proud tradition and culture. Though not rich his parents inculcated in him a love of music and of books. His father, a stonemason and fine craftsman, was also a fine musician. Hardy also played the violin and often entertained at village parties and gatherings. Music was almost a passion in his life and it even permeated his novels and poetry. (In *Far from the Madding Crowd*, Gabriel Oak plays the flute and Bathsheba sings.) Hardy's mother was a great lover of books.

Hardy was a good student, deeply interested in Greek and Latin, and read widely in English literature. He was a self-taught scholar as his parents could not afford a university education for their son. He was unhappy on account of this. He was not inclined towards science subjects. He was sent to be an apprentice with the local architect, John Hicks, who was an educated man and whose office was friendly. The dialect poet William Barnes had his school next door. Hardy had exciting literary and philosophical discussions with Barnes and with also his fellow draughtsmen. He was strongly influenced by Henry Bastow, a Baptist, and Greek scholar.

After completing his training with Hicks, Hardy worked for some time in the same office. In 1862 he decided to go to London. He secured a position as an assistant architect and draughtsman with Arthur Blomfield and specialised in ecclesiastical architecture. Hardy won medals for his design and innovative ideas. 'Architects and architecture were to figure prominently in Hardy's fiction most notably in *A Laodicean*'. (G. Harvey)

Hardy the young man in London was witness to the building of the raised stone structure on the banks of the Thames and the Charing Cross Railway Bridge. He participated actively in the cultural life of the capital. He attended lectures and dances, and saw Shakespearean plays. In London he met poets and scholars like T. H. Huxley, Swinburne, and Robert Browning. By 1867 he had begun to write poetry. He visited art exhibitions and art galleries and read books on politics and philosophy. It was Horace Moule, son of the vicar of Fordington (Dorchester) who stimulated and shaped his intellectual life and introduced him to the writings of Henry Newman. Though Hardy's family was Anglican, his readings of Mill, Comte, and other thinkers made him an agnostic.

Hardy realised that his fortune lay in writing. His poems of 1865–1866 were romantic in nature and may have been influenced by the early Tennyson and even Browning. He may have been inspired by his friendship with Eliza Nicholls and her sister Mary Jane in the 'She to Him' series of poems, and in the Wessex poems.

Hardy decided to leave London for reasons of health and overwork. Loneliness also made him depressed. His beliefs were being tested. He could not afford the much coveted university education and he decided to resign his post with Blomfield and return to Dorset, 'physically and emotionally exhausted.' He resumed work with John Hicks. It was mostly church restoration which he enjoyed. He realised that poetry could not make for an independent career and took to the novel. His first novel *The Poor Man and the Lady* (1867) had 'power and insight but was defective in form.'

In Dorset he met a young and beautiful school teacher Tryphena Sparks to whom he may have been engaged. Hardy continued his hand at writing novels. His second effort, *Desperate Remedies* (1870) was accepted for publication in the usual serial form, with a sensational plot of 'impersonation, illegitimacy, and murder' and it was not well-received. Only its rustic characters were commended.

In 1870 he went to Cornwall to renovate a church. There he met Emma Gifford, the sister-in-law of the Rector. Both fell in love with each other and enjoyed music and literary pursuits together.

His next novel *Under the Greenwood Tree* (1872) is a 'comedy of courtship' with rustic flavour. Reviews were favourable and back in London to do some designs of new schools Hardy wrote *A Pair of Blue Eyes* (1873), as a serial in *Tinsley's Magazine*. It had strong autobiographical elements. Emma was supportive of his efforts and he proposed to her. Her parents were not favourable of the match. However with the publication of *Far from the Madding Crowd* (1874), fame and money came Hardy's way. He married Emma in 1874 and then life was filled with happy moments and literary interludes. Hardy wrote *The Hand of Ethelberta* (1875) followed by *The Return of the Native* (1878). There are autobiographical notes informed by his childhood experiences of nature and the rural community.

For professional reasons Hardy decided to stay near London. Emma was resentful of Hardy's preoccupation with his work and neglect of her. She was also plagued by ill-health, and their childlessness worried them. However Hardy's professional status was gaining recognition. He wrote *The Trumpet Major* (1880), a cheerful historical novel. This was followed by *A Laodicean* (1881), a love story in comic mode exploring the conflict between the ancient and the modern.

In September 1880, he visited Dorset and decided to buy a plot of land to build a house. It seemed appropriate that he should do so as the novelist of Wessex. He left London to settle near Dorchester and wrote 'Two on a Town' for the *Atlantic Magazine.* Hardy moved residence again as Emma was not satisfied with the social life at Winborne. His own house Max Gate which he designed, was being built and soon they moved in. His next novel *The Mayor of Casterbridge* (1886) appeared as a serial in *The Graphic.* It focuses on the psychological complexity of Michael Henchard who in a drunken fit sells his wife and later as mayor suffers retribution. It was truly a Wessex novel. However the reception was disappointing. In the same year *The Woodlanders* was published as a serial and was well received. His personal life was becoming difficult and he had to spend more time with his wife. He was now asked to write more short stories.

He wrote *Tess of the d'Urbervilles* for *The Graphic* in 1891. It was based on personal experience and was controversial and popular. Hardy's final great novel *Jude the Obscure* in which he expresses society's hypocrisies, drew harsh reviews. Hardy decided to stop writing novels. This saw the emergence of the poet.

Emma's health deteriorated over a period of time. In November 1912, she died of heart failure. This plunged Hardy in grief and for some time he was in an emotional turmoil. His friendship with Florence Dugdale helped him stabilise and they married in 1914. In spite of failing health, Hardy remained active and wrote poems and published them. Many accolades came his way. His last poem was 'He resolves to say no more.' After a short illness and progressive weakness, Hardy suffered a heart attack and died on 11 January 1928. He was given a public funeral and his ashes were buried in Westminister Abbey. Edmund Gosse's tribute is worth quoting: 'The throne is vacant and literature is greatly bereaved . . . His modesty, his serenity, his equipoise of taste combined with the extraordinary persistence of his sympathy make him an object of affectionate respect to young and old alike.'

Far from the Madding Crowd: Title and Publication

The title 'Far from the Madding crowd' is taken from Thomas Gray's 'Elegy on a Country Churchyard':

'Far from the madding crowd's ignoble strife
Their sober wishes never learned to stray;
Along the cool, sequestered vale of life
They kept the noiseless tenor of their way.'

Suggestive of peace and contentment, the landscape of the novel is essentially the countryside—specifically Hardy's Wessex. The simplicity and the charm of the rustics are sensitively portrayed. The action of the novel never moves out of the village. The ills of urban mechanisation have not entered the life of the farmers. There is no painful unemployment or inhumanity. The novel is set in a 'golden period'—the barn is a symbol of the sanctity of work. Of course the social ills which would devastate an agrarian society are depicted but the gloom, despair, and pessimism of the later novels are not there. It is the idyllic pastoral that prevails.

After a few setbacks, with the success of *Under the Greenwood Tree* (1872), it was Leslie Stephen (1832–1904), editor of *The Cornhill Magazine,* who wrote to Hardy indicating that he would like to use his work. The young Hardy replied that he had a pastoral tale in mind and gave its title. The main characters would be a young woman-farmer with her own farm to manage, a shepherd, and a soldier. Stephen was happy with the first four chapters and wanted to begin publishing in January 1874.

The first instalment of the novel was published in the January 1874 *Cornhill* issue. It appeared anonymously from January to December. It was then published in two volumes by Smith, Elden & Co. on 23rd November 1874 and sold well. In fact the author was mistaken to be George Eliot. Refuting this, Hardy asserted that 'she (George Eliot) had never touched the life of the fields' and was 'not a born storyteller by any means'.

Hardy's name as a novelist was by then well established and there were more offers. The reviews of this novel were laudatory and his descriptive power and poetic evocation of nature were highlighted. His personal life also saw much happiness and contentment with the financial and artistic success. The novel was translated into German, adapted to the stage, and has also been filmed.

Structure and plot of the novel

Far from the Madding Crowd is a simple love story set against a pastoral setting. Three men love the same woman. She marries the third, the second kills the third, and then she marries the first suitor. This is a bald and dull statement. But Hardy invests his characters—Gabriel Oak, Boldwood, Troy and Bathsheba Everdene—with inward qualities and distinct external appearance which make them unique as individuals. It is their interactions in their individual way, that form the action in the novel—action that is absorbing and suspenseful. And the telling of the tale makes it interesting for it is appropriate and satisfying. While serialisation in his day might have had its problems, Hardy tried his best to please the reader by varying the season and the mood in the narrative as and when appropriate.

The plot of the novel is simple and not complex or complicated. Gabriel Oak, a respectable farmer and an honest and simple man falls in love with Bathsheba Everdene, the local beauty. He does not appeal to her vanity—she turns him down and leaves the neighbourhood for Weatherbury. Oak is disappointed but carries on with his honest livelihood as a sheep farmer. Next, tragedy strikes when Oak's entire flock is driven off a cliff by an inexperienced sheep-dog and Oak is left with nothing but a huge debt to pay. He remains stoic as he goes in search of work first to Casterbridge and then to Weatherbury. By a strange coincidence he finds employment as a farmhand in Bathsheba's farm. Even though their social situations had now changed, Oak is content to work for Bathsheba and admire her from afar. Over the years he proves to be a loyal worker and a trustworthy friend. The dignified Farmer Boldwood begins to court Bathsheba seriously after receiving a valentine card from Bathsheba sent as a joke in a moment of light-hearted gaiety. It is at this moment also that the handsome young Sergeant Troy appears in Weatherbury and begins to woo Bathsheba with his flattery. Bathsheba finds herself utterly drawn to Troy and is in a state of heightened confusion. Boldwood gives in and steps down for Troy. Before long Troy and Bathsheba are married and Troy moves in as the new landlord. He has little regard for or interest in farm matters and begins to spend Bathsheba's money freely.

The sub-plot involves Sergeant Troy and Fanny Robin, Boldwood's ward and one of Bathsheba's workers on the farm. When Fanny goes missing, Bathsheba makes inquiries. She gathers that Fanny had gone off to where the soldiers are in the hope of marrying her soldier-boyfriend. This predates Bathsheba's meeting with Sergeant Troy. Troy had previously agreed to marry Fanny and had gone to the altar at All Saints' Church. Fanny had on the other hand made an appearance at All Souls' Church by mistake. The mistake cost her her marriage as Troy had abandoned her.

Fanny runs into Troy when he is returning from the farmers' market in the company of his wife, Bathsheba. Bathsheba does not recognise Fanny and Troy cleverly conceals the facts concerning his former relationship with her. Fanny is ill and impoverished and is on her way to the Casterbridge workhouse. The following day, Bathsheba receives word that Fanny had died in the workhouse. Bathsheba arranges for her body to be brought to the farm and for the funeral arrangements to be made. It is at this juncture that truths come to light and Troy's former relationship with Fanny is made public. Bathsheba who has been progressively despondent since her marriage to Troy is now shocked and deeply distressed.

Troy goes away in anguish and news reaches Bathsheba that he had been drowned. His clothes are returned to her. Boldwood makes a re-appearance and promises to wait for Bathsheba if she would agree to marry him after a decent interval of six years. Troy in the meantime had been saved by some sailors. After much wandering and reaching the shores of America, he returns to Weatherbury as part of a travelling circus group. Boldwood's Christmas-eve party given on account of Bathsheba brings about a meeting between Bathsheba and Troy. Troy had decided to return to Bathsheba and tries to force her to go with him. Boldwood is stirred to anger and confusion and shoots Troy. He later surrenders to the police and is given a prison sentence of life imprisonment. With Troy dead, and Boldwood out of the way, Bathsheba begins to take notice of Gabriel Oak who had stood by her in constancy all these years. She accepts when he proposes to her.

Character is central to the action, mainly the character of Bathsheba around whom the plot revolves. It is Bathsheba's activities and feelings that form the crux of the tale. If her story is the main plot, the minor plot is the life of the rustics. However their life in nature is networked with that of their mistress. They perform a choice function and are commentators and reporters. The rustic dialogue and the charm and the natural environment contribute to the plot progression. It is a masterstroke of Hardy that the happenings in the main plot such as the marriage of Bathsheba, are reported by a rustic.

The plot has been described as artificial and creaky with too many coincidences and much melodrama. This may be justified but in the final analysis it is this plot which has enabled Hardy to associate humankind with nature and its grandeur and how it is important that humans respect the rhythms of nature—the substructure of the pastoral creating the mood of the action.

The success of the novel has been attributed to the qualities of its characters. In studying character, the reader has to depend on what the author says about each, what the character does, and what others say about him/her. Sometimes the environment also contributes to the plot and character reading. One symbolic reading of the flashes of lightning in the storm-scene is that the truth of Bathsheba's situation is revealed to her. Character-interest dominates the novel.

Important Themes and Motifs

1. The theme of unrequited love

The love of one person for another that is not returned (or mutual) is called unrequited love. Even though it is Bathsheba and her three suitors who stand out in the plot, it is the love relationship that plays out between these characters that lend interest and complexity to the plot. Love is never a straightforward relationship in Hardy's novels. There are forces that work outside the lives of the characters—fate, destiny—that thwart the love relationship. Oftentimes the love of one character for another is not returned, or is returned after a period of time.

Gabriel Oak as a respectable farmer is attracted to Bathsheba and wishes to marry her but she is a haughty and flighty young woman who says she does not love him. When he loses his farm and his flock and moves away, he goes to Weatherbury (where he knows Bathsheba lives) to look for a job. Oak is employed by Bathsheba (who has inherited her uncle's farm) on account of his skills and remains as her shepherd, bailiff, protector, and loyal friend. He advises her when she is in trouble and supports her ventures without ever being sure that she would reciprocate his love for her.

Boldwood's feelings for Bathsheba can also be seen as an example of unrequited love. Bathsheba in a moment of frivolity sends the valentine sealed with the words 'Marry me' to Farmer Boldwood, a confirmed bachelor. Boldwood's passions are stirred and he becomes her suitor with hopes of marrying her. Bathsheba is unable to return his love as she had never had the same feelings for him. He even offers to wait for six years to marry her after Troy's supposed 'drowning' accident. Boldwood believes she is pliant enough and would agree to a marriage proposal given enough time to think about it.

Bathsheba's love for Troy is unrequited even though Troy flirts with her feelings and their relationship ends in marriage. Troy is opportunistic and uses the marriage with Bathsheba to establish himself as a farmer and derive benefits from her money. He mistreats her after marriage but she loves him deeply. The Fanny Robin incident leaves her extremely hurt and despondent. She faints on hearing that Troy had been drowned, and feels deep within that he would return one day and that she would wait for him.

The conflict and the tragedy in *Far from the Madding Crowd* arise from unrequited love.

2. Natural catastrophes in *Far From the Madding Crowd*

Hardy loved nature and the rustic simplicity of country-folk and has written about nature eloquently in all his novels. Hardy himself described the novel as a 'novel of character and environment'. Hardy's knowledge and observation of nature are evident in his descriptions. He gives detailed descriptions of the Wessex countryside, the farmers, the farm labourers/ farm hands, the corn exchange, shearing supper, the harvest supper and other activities of the rural folk. Hardy's rural folk live close to nature in such a way that they are significantly affected by natural catastrophes. This has a serious impact on the lives of the characters. The catastrophes are sometimes averted at the nick of time.

The first of the catastrophes affects Gabriel Oak directly. Oak loses his flock of two hundred sheep when an inexperienced sheep dog drives the sheep over the edge of a cliff into a chalk pit dug adjacent to his land. His hopes of being an independent farmer were instantly dashed. He had lost all his savings. The chapter shows Gabriel Oak as morally a strong person, and a practical person at that. His only comment is: 'Thank God I am not married: what would she have done in the poverty now coming upon me!'

The second of the catastrophes, a fire, occurs as Gabriel Oak enters Weatherbury. Oak had attended the hiring fair at Casterbridge but was not lucky enough to find a job there. He then found himself in neighbouring Weatherbury when he came upon the fire in a farmyard. A straw stack was on fire and burned furiously. The flames were in danger of reaching the wheat-rick nearby, putting the entire farm produce at risk. Gabriel Oak used all the resources at his disposal to put out the flames and save the harvested crops. It is when he is summoned to be thanked by the farmer that he comes face to face with his beloved Bathsheba Everdene, the owner of the farm. The scene draws attention to Oak's character and capabilities while moving the story forward to create a coincidental meeting between Oak and Bathsheba. Bathsheba had inherited her uncle's farm in Weatherbury.

The third catastrophe in the novel is a thunderstorm followed by heavy rain. Here again it is Gabriel Oak who comes to the rescue. 'I will help to my last effort the woman I have loved so dearly,' says Oak. Troy gives a harvest supper and dance and uses the occasion to celebrate his marriage to Bathsheba. A storm breaks out and Oak works through the night trying to save the newly harvested barley, corn, and wheat which would have been ruined if they had not been covered. He looks for assistance but Troy and the farm workers are drunk and asleep. He is partly assisted by Bathsheba who arrives on the scene, also anxious to save her harvest. The natural catastrophe brings out Oak's sense of responsibility while contrasting it with Troy's sense of abandon and recklessness. The scene also provides a forum for Oak and Bathsheba to meet. Important revelations are made as to what prompted Bathsheba to marry Troy so suddenly.

3. Hardy's use of coincidences in *Far from the Madding Crowd*

The futile struggle of humans against fate or destiny is central to an understanding of Hardy's world view. Even though Hardy was brought up a Christian and an Anglican, his reading in literature and philosophy made him innately pessimistic and led him to question the existence of God. What is predominantly present in his novels is the notion of man/woman as a passive victim in the hands of a severe and indifferent Fate, which is a brooding presence, almost like a Greek god on Mount Olympus. However hard the characters in the novels may strive for something, however intensely and passionately they may love, it is Fate or Destiny that determines the outcome. In *Far from the Madding Crowd,* if Bathsheba had not sent the valentine to Boldwood, if Fanny had not missed her wedding, the entire story would have been different. Hardy's characters are, as it were, in the clutches of Fate. The workings of Fate in Hardy's novels are implemented through the use of coincidences or accidental events. Some of the novels like *Tess of the d'Urbervilles,* are saturated with coincidences, leaving little room for individual will but others are less so.

In *Far from the Madding Crowd,* the coincidences add interest to the story and help to further the plot. They do not have the devastating consequences that are characteristic of coincidences in some of the tragic novels by Hardy. It is a sheer coincidence that the girl seated on the wagon that Gabriel Oak met earlier on the road, is the same girl (Bathsheba) who saves him from smoke and suffocation in his hut later. Again, Bathsheba had been gone for two months. Gabriel Oak goes to Casterbridge and on to Weatherbury looking for work. He chances upon a fire accident in a farm and helps to put it out. It is a coincidence that Bathsheba is the owner of the farm.

It is coincidence that causes the tragedy in Fanny Robin's life. She confuses All Saints' church and All Souls' church, thus ending up in the wrong church and missing her marriage ceremony. This causes a permanent breach between her and Sergeant Troy.

There is a coincidental meeting with Fanny Robin on the road, months later, when Troy and Bathsheba are returning from the

Farmers market. This is followed by Bathsheba's coincidental sighting of Fanny's golden lock of hair in Troy's watch-case.

The coincidences in *Far from the Madding Crowd* do not drastically change the course of events, as in *Tess of the D'Urbervilles*, but contribute to a better understanding of character and intensity of feeling.

Important Characters

Bathsheba is the central character. The whole novel deals with her emotional life as a woman with conflicting love interests, and her practical life as a level-headed farm manager. Her inexplicable playfulness may be an aberration as seen in the looking-glass episode, and in sending the valentine to Boldwood, or in teasing Oak. She is an educated, light-hearted beautiful girl who inherits her uncle's property and takes over as manager of the farm. And it is in the management of this sheep farm that she shows her ability and strength of character. She is on equal terms with the men around her and is capable of firm action as when dismissing her dishonest bailiff, or when disbursing wages, or doing business in the corn market. As a woman she is impulsive and her beauty makes her succumb to masculine attention. She rejects Oak but falls a prey to Troy's flattering advances and takes advantage of Boldwood's genuine feelings for her. She knows her faults, acknowledges them and later on treats Boldwood with sympathy but lightly. She recognises Boldwood's passionate love for her and refuses him as she did not love him. However when Troy was supposedly 'dead' she does entertain his suit. She recognises Gabriel Oak's striking qualities and employs him, and seeks his advice on personal and professional matters.

Courageous and determined, she never flinches in moments of crisis. Troy cites the sword exercise as an outstanding example of her pluck. More significant are her valiant efforts to assist Oak in protecting the harvest during the storm and the stoic manner in which she behaves when Troy is killed and she single-handedly prepares the body for burial—'She was of the stuff of which great men's mothers are made.' Bathsheba matures through her experiences.

Gabriel Oak, as the name symbolises, combines angelic goodness and strength and durability like the sturdy oak. Oak is a committed worker wishing to succeed in life. He is simple, straightforward and sometimes tactless as seen in his wooing of Bathsheba. Gentle and humane, his actions are characterised by kindness and generosity—he pays Bathsheba's toll fee, helps Fanny Robin and is genuinely upset when his sheep meet a tragic end. Gabriel is endowed with great physical strength and mental stamina. He is altruistic as seen in his efforts to save Bathsheba's farm produce. Hence his tenacity of purpose and courage are evident—he fights the farm fire single-handed. Where other characters may have wavered in their loyalty, Oak remains the same, always offering protection to Bathsheba. He is close to nature and sharing what the critic R. W. V. Elliott calls its 'timelessness'. Even when plagued by misfortune as in the loss of his sheep and of his position, he remains cheerful and accepts his situation with fortitude and philosophical resignation. He stays by Bathsheba's side and tries to save her every heartache as when he rubs out the words 'and child' on Fanny's coffin. It is not in his nature to condemn anyone—whether it is Troy or Boldwood. This is seen when he warns Bathsheba against Troy but does not reveal his infidelity to Fanny. He even sympathises with Boldwood. Hardy presents Gabriel as the ideal rustic and human being.

R. W. V. Elliott remarks of Troy: 'Troy for all his philandering nature is no villain . . . yet the sensuality of Troy and the superficiality of his feelings for Bathsheba are an important element in the novel. They provide a contrast for both the silent constancy of Gabriel's love and the passionate frenzy of Boldwood's.'

Troy was a handsome dashing young soldier, a man of attractive and easy ways, an adroit swordsman and easily 'any woman's man'. He was a well-educated individual of middle-class origin, fluent in speech and flashing in manners. He could flatter with ease. He had no responsibility to the farming community even though he is quick to take on as farmer on his marriage to Bathsheba. On the night of the storm he is asleep after a drunken reverie indifferent to the state of the newly harvested crops. That he was unprincipled and materialistic is seen in his return to Bathsheba after the 'drowning act'. She was the owner of a farm and property while he was a poor adventurer-wanderer. The saving grace in his nature was probably his love for Fanny which however was manifest only after her death. His life of self-indulgence ends in violence when Boldwood shoots him for his brutish behaviour towards Bathsheba.

Farmer Boldwood spelt 'dignity' in all his actions till the valentine from Bathsheba turned his head. He was a handsome gentleman of forty respected by all. He was kind in his dealings with his shepherds and cared for them as is evident in his concern for Fanny. He remained a bachelor even at forty. 'His equilibrium disturbed, he was in extremity at once. If an emotion possessed him at all it ruled him . . . He was always hit mortally or he was missed.'

He was a man disposed towards melancholy and solitude. Introspective by nature, he soon became obsessed with the idea of possessing Bathsheba and a notion that she would be totally his with no occupation of her own. However his sense of propriety made him direct Bathsheba to go with Troy—this when Troy appeared immediately after Bathsheba had promised to marry Boldwood after the stipulated six years. However Troy's brutishness towards Bathsheba excited him enough to shoot him. Was this act testimony to his insanity? Boldwood was intensely jealous of Troy and over-possessive of Bathsheba and this might have triggered the killing. Boldwood's locked closet reveals dresses and jewellery bearing the name 'Bathsheba Boldwood' on each item. Boldwood surrendered to the police and his death sentence was changed to life imprisonment. That he is a tragic figure defeated in love and life contributes to the tragic tone in the novel which otherwise ends happily for Oak and Bathsheba.

Minor Characters

Fanny Robin makes few appearances in the story but her role is important as a connecting link between the major characters. A country girl who worked for both Boldwood and Bathsheba's uncle, Fanny ran away to marry her soldier-lover who was Troy. However the marriage did not take place due to a mistake on Fanny's part and she was abandoned. Oak helped her when she was down and out financially, and her letter to him showed her honesty and simplicity. She died in childbirth failing again to keep her appointment with Troy. Troy's efforts to make amends were in vain.

Lydia Smallbury was the aged malster's great-granddaughter and Bathsheba's personal maidservant and confidante. She is practical and dependable and is helpful to Bathsheba.

Lydia and the other rustics bring a certain mellowness and tranquillity to the action. They are calm and humble and respect nature. Their respect for each other, their simplicity and dignified bearing coupled with their patience and fortitude contribute to the appeal of the novel. In fact, besides the physical background, 'the social background made up of the numerous minor characters from the Wessex peasantry is of equal importance'.

Significant Techniques and Aspects of Style

Far from the Madding Crowd is Hardy's fourth novel but his first literary success. Its success has largely been attributed to Hardy's characterisation of Gabriel Oak, Bathsheba, Boldwood, and Troy, but also to his description of rural life and its people. In the novel one begins to see Hardy's growing taste for tragedy as the characters Fanny, Troy and Boldwood, all come to a tragic end. Also, an unfortunate accident results in Gabriel Oak's tragedy of losing his entire flock of sheep and his farm. The plot takes the reader through Bathsheba's love entanglements until she comes to a self-awakening. Her vanity and her physical attraction for Troy result in a whirlwind marriage. It is an unhappy marriage with prospects of financial ruin on Bathsheba's part, as she soon discovers. She is rescued only by Troy's death. The valentine incident leads to her feelings of guilt and entanglement with Boldwood. In the end she comes to the realisation that it is Gabriel Oak who has stood by her in good and bad times, and is her loyal friend and true companion.

Hardy presents a vivid picture of rural England and the joys and sufferings of rural people in the novel. There are convincing pictures of the corn exchange, of sheep shearing, 'lambing of the ewes', of the farmers' market, and the harvest supper. There is sympathy and humour in Hardy's presentation of the rustics, their speech and their idiosyncratic behaviour. There are detailed descriptions of Gabriel Oak and the interior of his hut in the early chapters. Oak is a practical, straightforward, unsophisticated farmer. Rustics are also used at key points in the story. It is Cain Ball, one of the rustics who reports the important news of Bathsheba's visit to Bath to see Troy. It is Joseph Poorgrass who is given the responsibility of conveying Fanny's corpse to Bathsheba's farm.

That nature could be peaceful and beautiful but also violent and destructive are seen in the novel. There is a vivid description of the storm in chapter 31, and Oak's devotion to duty. The difference between Troy and Oak is brought out symbolically on the night of the storm. As the lightning flashes, Bathsheba 'unconsciously realises the uselessness of one and the worth of the other'. Oak works all night to save his mistress's newly harvested crops. Troy, on the other hand, is in a state of drunken slumber after a night of festivity with the farmhands. Day and night are also used as symbols to convey the nature of Bathsheba's relationship with Oak and Troy. Bathsheba meets Oak in broad daylight signifying an open, honest, and uncomplicated relationship. Her meeting with Troy in the fir plantation, on the other hand, is in the shade of night. It also turns out to be a dark and intense relationship characterised by deceit.

R. W. V. Elliott points out that Hardy uses dialogue as an instrument of characterisation and narrative. Apart from the speech of the rustics which has local flavour and colour, the major characters in the novel reveal themselves through their speech. Troy is extremely confident in his demeanour, his speech is full of flattery and deceit particularly when he is talking to women. Bathsheba is so overcome by her feelings for Troy that she becomes strangely tongue-tied when she is with him, and totally inarticulate. Gabriel Oak has a distinctive, slow and unhurried manner of speaking, in keeping with his character.

Orient BlackSwan Drama Classics

Orient BlackSwan Drama Classics, with Professor S. Viswanathan as General Editor, is a series from Orient BlackSwan that fulfils the long-felt need of Indian students and teachers for a comprehensive Indian edition of drama classics in English. Edited and annotated with scholarly expertise and meticulous care by eminent professors and specialists in the field, each edition provides a rich understanding and appreciation of the play in easily comprehensible language.

Highlights of this series:

- A ***General Introduction*** which provides the cultural and historical background for the drama of the period and a brief biography of the playwright.
- An ***Introduction to the Play*** which discusses the theme, the structure and the plot. It also includes a comprehensive critical study and a brief stage history of the play.
- ***Detailed annotations*** which are provided at the bottom of each page to facilitate referencing.
- ***Suggestions for Further Reading*** which helps students acquire a wide understanding of the play.
- ***Topics for Discussion*** which initiates classroom analysis and study.

Titles in this series

1. The Tempest: *William Shakespeare*
2. The Tragedy of Julius Caesar: *William Shakespeare*
3. The First Part of Henry the Fourth: *William Shakespeare*
4. As You Like It: *William Shakespeare*
5. The Duchess of Malfi: *John Webster*
6. Othello, Moor of Venice: *William Shakespeare*
7. Measure for Measure: *William Shakespeare*
8. Hamlet, Prince of Denmark: *William Shakespeare*

CHAPTER ONE

DESCRIPTION OF FARMER OAK—AN INCIDENT

When Farmer Oak smiled, the corners of his mouth spread till they were within an unimportant distance of his ears, his eyes were reduced to chinks, and diverging wrinkles appeared round them.

His Christian name was Gabriel, and on working days he was a young man of sound judgment, easy motions, proper dress and general good character. On Sundays he was a man of misty views, rather given to postponing, and hampered by his best clothes and umbrella.

Oak's appearance in his old clothes was most peculiarly his own. He wore a low-crowned felt hat, spread out at the base by tight jamming upon the head for security in high winds, and a coat like Dr Johnson's; his lower extremities being encased in ordinary leather leggings and boots emphatically large.

But some thoughtful persons might have regarded Gabriel Oak in other aspects than these. In his face one might notice that many of the hues and curves of youth had tarried on to manhood; there even remained some relics of the boy. His height and breadth would have been sufficient to make his presence imposing, had they been exhibited with due consideration. But Oak walked unassumingly, and with a faintly perceptible bend, yet distinct from a bowing of the shoulders.

He had just reached the time of life at which 'young' is ceasing to be the prefix of 'man' in speaking of one. He was at the brightest period of masculine growth, for his intellect and his emotions were clearly separated, and he had not yet arrived at the stage wherein they become united again, in the character of prejudice, by the influence of a wife and family. In short, he was twenty-eight, and a bachelor.

The field he was in this morning sloped to a ridge called Norcombe Hill. Casually glancing over the hedge, Oak saw coming down the incline before him an ornamental spring waggon, painted yellow and gaily marked, drawn by two horses, a waggoner walking alongside. On the apex of the whole sat a woman, young and attractive: It was a fine morning, and the sun lighted up to a scarlet glow the crimson jacket she wore, and painted a soft lustre upon her bright face and dark hair.

Gabriel had not beheld the sight for more than half a minute, when the vehicle was brought to a standstill just beneath his eyes.

'The tailboard of the waggon is gone, Miss,' said the waggoner.

'Then I heard it fall,' said the girl, in a soft, though not particularly low voice. 'I heard a noise when we were coming up the hill.'

'I'll run back.'

The waggoner's steps sank fainter and fainter in the distance. The handsome girl waited for some time idly in her place. Then she looked attentively downwards at an oblong package tied in paper. She turned her head; the waggoner was not yet in sight. At length she drew the article into her lap and untied the paper covering. A small looking-glass was disclosed in which she proceeded to survey herself attentively. She parted her lips and smiled. She did not adjust her hat or pat her hair, or press a dimple into shape. She simply observed herself as a fair product of Nature.

The waggoner's steps were heard returning. She put the glass in the paper and the whole again into its place.

When the waggon had passed on, Gabriel followed it to the turnpike-gate some way beyond the bottom of the hill where it now halted for the payment of toll. He heard a dispute. It was a difference concerning twopence between the persons with the waggon and the man at the toll-bar.

"Mis'ess's niece is upon the top of the things, and she says that's enough that I've offered ye, you great miser, and she won't pay any more.' These were the waggoner's words.

'Very well; then mis'ess's niece can't pass,' said the turnpike-keeper, closing the gate.

Oak looked from one to the other of the disputants. There was something in the tone of twopence remarkably insignificant. 'Here, he said, stepping forward and handing twopence to the gatekeeper; 'let the young woman pass.' He looked up at her then: she heard his words, and looked down. She carelessly glanced over him, and told her man to drive on.

The gatekeeper surveyed the retreating vehicle. That's a handsome maid,' he said to Oak.

'But she has her faults,' said Gabriel perhaps a little piqued by the comely traveller's indifference. 'And the greatest of them is—'Well, what it is always—vanity.'

CHAPTER TWO

NIGHT – THE FLOCK

It was nearly midnight on the eve of St Thomas's, the shortest day in the year. A desolating wind wandered from the north over the hill whereon Oak had watched the yellow waggon and its occupant in the sunshine of a few days earlier.

The sky was clear. Suddenly an unexpected series of sounds began to be heard. They had a clearness which was to be found nowhere in the wind, and a sequence which was to be found nowhere in nature. They were the notes of Farmer Oak's flute.

The tune came from a shepherd's hut which stood on little wheels, which raised its floor about a foot from the ground. Such shepherds' huts are dragged into the fields when the lambing season comes on, to shelter the shepherd in his enforced nightly attendance.

It was only latterly that people had begun to call Gabriel 'Farmer' Oak. During the twelvemonth preceding this time he had been enabled by sustained efforts of industry and chronic good spirits to leave the small sheep-farm of which Norcombe Hill was a portion, and stock it with two hundred sheep. Previously he had been a bailiff for a short time, and earlier still a shepherd only.

This venture, unaided and alone, with an advance of sheep not yet paid for, was a critical juncture with Gabriel Oak. The first movement in his new progress was the lambing of his ewes, and sheep having been his speciality from his youth, he wisely refrained from deputing the task of tending them at this season to a hireling or a novice.

The flute-playing ceased. A rectangular space of light appeared in the side of the hut, and in the opening the outline of Farmer Oak's figure. He carried a lantern in his hand, and closing the door behind him came forward and busied himself about this nook of the field for nearly twenty minutes.

The ring of the sheep-bell, which had been silent during his absence, recommenced. This continued till Oak withdrew again from the flock. He returned to the hut, bringing in his arms a new-born lamb.

The little speck of life he placed on a wisp of hay before the small stove. Oak extinguished the lantern by blowing into it and then pinching the snuff, the cot being lighted by a candle suspected by a twisted wire. A rather hard couch, formed of a few corn sacks thrown carelessly down, covered half the floor of this little habitation, and here the young man stretched himself along, and closed his eyes. In about the time a person unaccustomed to bodily labour would have decided upon which side to lie, Farmer Oak was asleep.

CHAPTER THREE

A GIRL ON HORSEBACK – CONVERSATION

The sluggish day began to break. Oak went into the plantation. He heard the steps of a horse at the foot of the hill, and soon there appeared in view an auburn pony with a girl on its back. She was the young heroine of the yellow waggon and looking-glass: the woman who owed him twopence. Gabriel returned to his hut, and peeped through the loophole in the direction of the rider's approach.

The path she came by was not a bridle-path—merely a pedestrian's track, and the boughs spread horizontally at a height not greater than seven feet above the ground, which made it impossible to ride erect beneath them. The girl, who wore no riding-habit, looked around for a moment, as if to assure herself that all humanity was out of view, then dexterously dropped backwards flat upon the pony's back, her head over its tail, her feet against its shoulders, and her eyes to the sky. The tall lank pony seemed used to such doings, and ambled along unconcerned. Thus she passed under the level boughs.

The performer seemed quite at home anywhere between a horse's head and its tail, and the necessity for this abnormal attitude having ceased with the passage of the plantation, she began to adopt another, even more obviously convenient than the first. She had no side-saddle, and it was very apparent that a firm seat upon the smooth leather beneath her was unattainable sideways. Springing to her accustomed perpendicular, and satisfying herself that nobody was in sight, she seated herself in the manner demanded by the saddle, though hardly expected of the woman and trotted off.

Oak was amused, perhaps a little astonished, and went again among his ewes.

Five mornings and evenings passed. One afternoon it began to freeze, and the frost increased with evening. Oak entered his hut and heaped more fuel upon the stove. The wind came in at the bottom of the door, and to prevent it Oak laid a sack there and wheeled the cot round a little more to the south.

There were two ventilating holes—one on each side of the hut. Gabriel had always known that when the fire was lighted and the door closed one of these must be kept open—that chosen being always on the side away from the wind. The farmer considered that he would first sit down, leaving both closed for a minute or two, till the temperature of the hut was a little raised. He sat down.

His head began to ache in an unwonted manner and he fell asleep, without having performed the necessary preliminary.

How long he remained unconscious Gabriel never knew. During the first stages of his return to perception peculiar deeds seemed to be in course of enactment. His dog was howling, his head was aching fearfully—somebody was pulling him about, hands were loosening his neckerchief.

On opening his eyes he found that evening had sunk to dusk. The young girl with the remarkably pleasant lips and white teeth was beside him. More than this—astonishingly more—his head was upon her lap, his face and neck were disagreeably wet, and her fingers were unbuttoning his collar.

"Whatever is the matter?" said Oak vacantly.

She seemed to experience mirth.

'Nothing now,' she answered, 'since you are not dead. It is a wonder you were not suffocated in this hut of yours.'

'Ah, the hut!' murmured Gabriel. I gave ten pounds for that hut. But I'll sell it, and sit under thatched hurdles, and curl up to sleep in a lock of straw!' Gabriel, by way of emphasis, brought down his fist upon the floor.

She made him sit up, and then Oak began wiping his face and shaking himself. 'How can I thank 'ee?' he said at last gratefully, some of the natural, rusty red having returned to his face.

'Oh, never mind that,' said the girl, smiling.

"How did you find me?"

'I heard your dog howling and scratching at the door of the hut when I came to the milking. The dog saw me, and jumped over to me, and laid hold of my skirt. I came across and looked around the hut the very first thing to see if the slides were closed. My uncle has a hut like this one, and I have heard him tell his shepherd not to go to sleep without leaving a slide open. I opened the door, and there you were like dead,'

'I believe you saved my life Miss—I don't know your name. I know your aunt's but not yours.'

'You can inquire at my aunt's—she will tell you.'

'My name is Gabriel Oak.'

'And mine isn't. You seem fond of yours in speaking it so decisively. Gabriel Oak.'

'You see, it is the only one I shall ever have, and I must make the most of it.'

'I always think mine sounds odd and disagreeable.'

'I should think you might soon get a new one.'

'Mercy!—how many opinions you keep about you concerning other people, Gabriel Oak.'

'Well, Miss—excuse the words—I thought you would like them. But I can't match you, I know, in mapping out my mind upon my tongue. I never was very clever in my inside. But I thank you. Come, give me your hand!'

She hesitated, somewhat disconcerted at Oak's old-fashioned earnest conclusion to a dialogue lightly carried on. 'Very well,' she said, and gave him her hand.

Oak held it long, indeed curiously long.

'There—that's long enough,' said she, though without pulling it away. 'But I suppose you are thinking you would like to kiss it? You may if you want to.'

'I wasn't thinking of any such thing,' said Gabriel simply; 'but I will—'

'That you won't!' She snatched back her hand.

Gabriel felt himself guilty of want of tact.

'Now find out my name,' she said teasingly; and withdrew.

CHAPTER FOUR

GABRIEL'S RESOLVE – THE VISIT – THE MISTAKE

This well-favoured and comely girl soon made appreciable inroads upon the emotional constitution of young Farmer Oak. By making inquiries he found that the girl's name was Bathsheba Everdene. Gabriel had reached a pitch of existence he never could have anticipated a short time before. He liked saying 'Bathsheba' as a private enjoyment instead of whistling; turned over his taste to black hair, though he had sworn by brown ever since he was a boy. He said to himself, 'I'll make her my wife, or upon my soul I shall be good for nothing!'

All this while he was perplexing himself about an errand on which he might consistently visit the cottage of Bathsheba's aunt.

He found his opportunity in the death of a ewe, mother of a living lamb. On a fine January morning, Oak put the lamb into a respectable Sunday basket, and stalked across the fields to the house of Mrs Hurst, the aunt.

Bathsheba was out.

'Will you come in, Mr Oak?' said Mrs Hurst.

'Oh, thank 'ee,' said Gabriel, following her to the fireplace. 'I've brought a lamb for Miss Everdene. I thought she might like one to rear; girls do.'

'She might,' said Mrs Hurst musingly; 'though she's only a visitor here. If you will wait a minute Bathsheba will be in.'

'Yes, I will wait,' said Gabriel, sitting down. 'The lamb isn't really the business I came about, Mrs Hurst. In short, I was going to ask her if she'd like to be married. Because if she would I should be very glad to marry her. D'ye know if she's got any other young man hanging about her at all?'

'Let me think,' said Mrs Hurst . . . . 'Yes—bless you, ever so many young men. You see, Farmer Oak, she's so good-looking, and an excellent scholar besides. Not that her young men ever come here—but, Lord, she must have a dozen!'

'That's unfortunate,' said Farmer Oak. 'I'm only an everyday sort of man, and my only chance was in being the first comer . . . Well, there's no use in my waiting, for that was all I came about: so I'll take myself off home-along, Mrs Hurst.'

When Gabriel had gone about two hundred yards he heard a 'hoi-hoi!' uttered behind him. He looked round, and saw a girl racing after him, waving a white handkerchief.

Oak stood still—and the runner drew nearer. It was Bathsheba Everdene.

'Farmer Oak—I—' she said, pausing for want of breath, panting like a robin, her face red and moist from exertions. 'I didn't know you had come to ask to have me, or I should have come in from the garden instantly. I ran after you to say—that my aunt made a mistake in sending you away from courting me.'

Gabriel expanded. 'I'm sorry to have made you run so fast, my dear,' he said, with a grateful sense of favours to come. 'Wait a bit till you've found your breath.'

'—It was quite a mistake—aunt's telling you I had a young man already,' Bathsheba went on. 'I haven't a sweetheart at all and I thought that it was such a pity to send you away thinking that I had several.'

'Really and truly I am glad to hear that!' said Farmer Oak, smiling one of his long special smiles, and blushing with gladness. He held out his hand to take hers. Directly he seized it she put it behind her, so that it slipped through his fingers like an eel.

'I have a nice snug little farm,' said Gabriel, with half a degree less assurance than when he had seized her hand.

'Yes; you have.'

'A man has advanced me money to begin with, but still, I will soon be paid off. He continued: 'When we be married, I am quite sure I can work twice as hard as I do now.'

'Why Farmer Oak,' she said, looking at him with rounded eyes. 'I never said I was going to marry you.'

'Well—that is a tale!' said Oak with dismay. 'To run after anybody like this, and then say you don't want him!'

'*Indeed,* I hadn't time to think before starting whether I wanted to marry or not, for you'd have been gone over the hill.'

'Come,' said Gabriel, freshening again; 'think a minute or two. I'll wait a while, Miss Everdene. Will you marry me? Do, Bathsheba. I love you far more than common!'

She was silent a while . . . then she decisively turned to him.

'No; 'tis no use,' she said. 'I don't want to marry you. I've tried hard all the time I've been thinking; for a marriage would be very nice in one sense. People would talk about me and think I had won my battle, and I should feel triumphant, and all that. What I mean is that I shouldn't mind being a bride at a wedding, if I could be one without having a husband. But since a woman can't show off in that way by herself, I shan't marry—at least yet.'

'Upon my heart and soul I don't know what a maid can say stupider than that,' said Oak. 'But dearest,' he continued in a palliative voice, 'don't be like it!' Oak sighed a deep honest sigh: 'Why won't you have me?' he appealed.

'Because I don't love you.'

'But I love you—and, as for myself, I am content to be liked.'

'O Mr Oak—that's very fine! You'd get to despise me.'

'Never,' said Mr Oak, 'I shall do one thing in this life—one thing certain—that is, love you, and long for you, and keep *wanting* you till I die.' His voice had a genuine pathos now, and his large brown hands perceptibly trembled.

'It seems dreadfully wrong not to have you when you feel so much!' she said with a little distress, and looking hopelessly around for some means of escape from her moral dilemma.

Oak cast his eyes down the field in a way implying that it was useless to attempt argument.

'Mr Oak,' she said, with luminous distinctness and common sense, 'I have hardly a penny in the world. You are a farmer just beginning, and you ought, in common prudence, to marry a woman with money, who would stock a larger farm for you than you have now.'

Gabriel looked at her with a little surprise and much admiration.

'That's the very thing I had been thinking myself!' he naively said.

Bathsheba was decidedly disconcerted. 'Well then why did you come and disturb me?'

'I can't do what I think would be—wise.'

'You have made an admission *now*, Mr Oak,' she exclaimed with hauteur, and rocking her head disdainfully. 'After that, do you think I could marry you? Not if I know it.'

He broke in passionately: 'But don't mistake me like that! Because I am open enough to own what every man in my shoes would have thought of, you make your colours come up your face and get crabbed with me. That about you not being good enough for me is nonsense. You speak like a lady and your uncle at Weatherbury is, I've heerd, a large farmer. May I call in the evening, or will you walk along with me o' Sundays? I don't want you to make up your mind at once, if you'd rather not.'

'No—no—I cannot. Don't press me any more—don't. I don't love you—so 'twould be ridiculous,' she said, with a laugh.

No man likes to see his emotions the sport of a merry-go-round of skittishness. 'Very well,' said Oak firmly. 'Then I'll ask you no more.'

CHAPTER FIVE

DEPARTURE OF BATHSHEBA—A PASTORAL TRAGEDY

The news one day reached Gabriel that Bathsheba Everdene had left the neighbourhood. It appeared that she had gone to a place called Weatherbury, more than twenty miles off, but in what capacity—whether as a visitor or permanently, he could not discover.

Gabriel had two dogs. George, the elder, though old, was clever and trustworthy still. The young dog, George's son, might possibly have been the image of his mother, for there was not much resemblance between him and George. He was learning the sheep-keeping business, so as to follow on at the flock when the other should die, but had got no further than the rudiments as yet—still finding an insuperable difficulty in distinguishing between doing a thing well enough and doing it too well.

Thus much for the dogs. On the further side of Norcombe Hill was a chalk-pit. Two hedges converged upon it in the form of a V, but without quite meeting. The narrow opening left, which was immediately over the brow of the pit, was protected by a rough railing.

One night, when Farmer Oak had returned to his house believing there would be no further necessity for his attendance on the down, he called as usual to the dogs. Only one responded—old George; the other could not be found, either in the house, lane, or garden. Gabriel then went indoors to the luxury of a bed, which latterly he had only enjoyed on Sundays.

To the shepherd, the note of the sheep-bell, like the ticking of the clock to other people, is a sound that only makes itself noticed by ceasing or altering in some unusual manner from the well-known idle tinkle which signifies to the accustomed ear, however distant, that all is well in the fold. In the solemn calm of the awakening morn that note was heard by Gabriel, beating with unusual violence and rapidity. The experienced ear of Oak knew the sound he now heard to be caused by the running of the flock with great velocity.

He jumped out of bed, dressed, tore down the lane through a foggy dawn, and ascended the hill. The fifty forward ewes were kept apart from those among which the fall of lambs would be later, there being two hundred of the latter class in Gabriel's flock. These two hundred seemed to have absolutely vanished from the hill. Gabriel called at the top of his voice the shepherd's call:

'Ovey, ovey, ovey!'

Not a single bleat. He went to the hedge; a gap had been broken through it, and in the gap were the footprints of the sheep. He followed through the hedge. They were not in the plantation. He called again but no sheep. He passed through the trees and along the ridge of the hill. On the extreme summit where the ends of the two converging hedges of which we have spoken were stopped short by meeting the brow of the chalk-pit, he saw the younger dog standing against the sky—dark and motionless.

A horrible conviction darted through Oak. With a sensation of the bodily faintness he advanced: at one point the rails were broken through, and there he saw the footprints of his ewes. Oak looked over the precipice. The ewes lay dead and dying at its foot—a heap of two hundred mangled carcases, representing in their condition just now at least two hundred more.

Oak was an intensely humane man. His first feeling now was one of pity for the untimely fate of these gentle ewes and their unborn lambs.

It was a second to remember another phase of the matter. The sheep were not insured. All the savings of a frugal life had been dispersed at a blow; his hopes of being an independent farmer were laid down low—possibly forever.

It was as remarkable as it was characteristic that the one sentence he uttered was in thankfulness:—

'Thank God I am not married: what would *she* have done in the poverty now coming upon me!'

As far as could be learnt it appeared that the poor young dog had collected all the ewes into a corner, driven the timid creatures through the hedge, across the upper field, and over the edge.

Gabriel's farm had been stocked by a dealer—on the strength of Oak's promising look and character—who was receiving a percentage from the farmer till such time as the advance should be cleared off. Oak found that the value of stock, plant, and implements which were really his own would be about sufficient to pay his debts, leaving himself a free man with the clothes he stood up in, and nothing more.

CHAPTER SIX

THE FAIR – THE JOURNEY – THE FIRE

Two months passed away. We are brought on to a day in February, on which was held the yearly statute or hiring fair in the country-town of Casterbridge.

At one end of the street stood from two to three hundred blithe and hearty labourers waiting upon Chance. Among these, carters and waggoners were distinguished by having a piece of whip-cord twisted round their hats; thatchers wore a fragment of woven straw; shepherds held their sheep-crooks in their hands; and thus the situation required was known to the hirers at a glance.

In the crowd was an athletic young fellow of somewhat superior appearance to the rest.

Gabriel was paler now. His eyes were more meditative, and his expression was more sad. He had sunk from his modest elevation, but there was left to him a dignified calm he had never before known.

In the morning a regiment of cavalry had left the town, and Gabriel almost wished that he had joined them and gone off to serve his country. He was weary of standing in the market-place.

All the farmers seemed to be wanting shepherds. Sheep-tending was Gabriel's speciality. He decided to offer himself in some other capacity than that of bailiff. He went to a smith's shop and a shepherd's crook was made. He stood again on the kerb of the pavement as a shepherd, crook in hand.

Now that Oak had turned himself into a shepherd it seemed that bailiffs were most in demand. He wished he had not nailed up his colours as a shepherd, but had laid himself out for anything in the whole cycle of labour that was required in the fair.

It grew dusk. Some merry men were whistling and singing by the corn-exchange. Gabriel drew out his flute which he carried and began to play 'Jockey to the Fair' in the style of a man who had never known a moment's sorrow. The sound of the well-known notes cheered his own heart as well as those of the loungers. He played on with spirit, and in half an hour had earned in pence what was a small fortune to a destitute man.

By making inquiries he learnt that there was another fair at Shottsford the next day.

Bathsheba had probably left Weatherbury long before this time, but the place had enough interest attaching to it to lead Oak to choose Shottsford as his next field of inquiry, because it lay in the Weatherbury quarter. Oak resolved to sleep at Weatherbury that night on his way to Shottsford, and struck out at once into the high road which had been recommended as the direct route to the village in question.

By the time he had walked three or four miles every shape in the landscape had assumed a uniform hue of blackness. He could just discern ahead of him a waggon, drawn up under a great overhanging tree by the roadside.

He found there were no horses attached to it. The waggon, from its position, seemed to have been left there for the night. Gabriel sat down on the shafts of the vehicle.

Eating his last slices of bread and ham, and drinking from the bottle of cider he had taken the precaution to bring with him, he got into the lonely waggon. Here he spread half of the hay as a bed, and, as well as he could in the darkness, pulled the other half over him by way of bed-clothes, covering himself entirely, and fell asleep.

On somewhat suddenly awaking, Oak found the waggon was in motion. He then distinguished voices in conversation coming from the forepart of the waggon. His concern led him to peer cautiously from the hay, and the first sight he beheld was the stars above him. Gabriel concluded that it must be about nine o'clock. There were now apparently close upon Weatherbury, and not to alarm the speakers unnecessarily Gabriel slipped out of the waggon unseen.

He turned to an opening in the hedge, which he found to be a gate. Mounting thereon he was meditating whether to seek a cheap lodging in the village, or to ensure a cheaper one by lying under some hay or corn stack, when he noticed an unusual light, about half a mile distant. Something was on fire.

Gabriel made across the field in the direction of the fire.

The fire was issuing from a long straw-stack, which was so far gone as to preclude a possibility of saving it. A scroll of smoke blew aside and revealed a wheat-rick in startling juxtaposition with the decaying one, and behind this a series of others composing the main corn produce of the farm.

Gabriel leapt over the hedge. The first man he came to was running about in a great hurry, as if his thoughts were several yards in advance of his body.

'O, man—fire, fire! O Mark Clark—come! And you, Billy Smallbury—and you, Maryann Money—and you, Jan Coggan, and Matthew there!' Other figures now appeared behind this shouting man and Gabriel found that he was in a great company—hard at work with a remarkable confusion of purpose.

'Stop the draught under the wheat-rick!' cried Gabriel to those nearest to him. If the fire once got under this stack, all would be lost.

'Get a tarpaulin—quick!' said Gabriel.

A rick-cloth was brought, and they hung it like a curtain across the channel. The flames immediately ceased to go under the bottom of the corn-stack, and stood up vertical.

'Stand here with a bucket of water and keep the cloth wet,' said Gabriel again.

The flames, now driven upwards, began to attack the angles of the huge roof covering the wheat stack.

'A ladder,' cried Gabriel.

'The ladder was against the straw-rick and it burnt to a cinder,' said a spectre-like form in the smoke.

Oak seized the cut ends of the sheaves, and digging in his feet and occasionally sticking in the stem of his sheep-crook he clambered up. He at once sat astride the very apex, and began with his crook to beat off the fiery fragments which had lodged thereon, shouting to the others to get him a bough and a ladder, and some water.

On the ground the groups of villagers were still occupied in doing all they could to keep down the conflagration, which was not much. Round the corner of the largest stack, out of the direct rays of the fire, stood a pony, bearing a young woman on its back. By her side was another woman, on foot.

The young woman looked anxiously around.

'Do you think the barn is safe?' she said.

'D'ye think the barn is safe, Jan Coggan?' said the second woman, passing on the question to the nearest man in that direction.

'Safe now—I think so. If this rick had gone the barn would have followed. 'Tis that bold shepherd up there that have done the most good—he sitting on the top o'rick.'

'He does work hard,' said the young woman on horseback, looking up at Gabriel through her thick woollen veil. 'I wish he was shepherd here. Don't any of you know his name?'

'Never heard the man's name in my life, or seen his form afore.'

The fire was dying out, and Gabriel made as if to descend.

'Maryann,' said the girl on horseback, 'go to him as he comes down, and say that the farmer wishes to thank him for the great service he has done.'

Maryann stalked off towards the rick and met Oak at the foot of the ladder. She delivered her message.

'Where is your master the farmer?' asked Gabriel, kindling with the idea of getting employment that seemed to strike him now.

''Tisn't a master; 'tis a mistress, shepherd, and a rich one too!' said a bystander. 'Lately' 'a came here from a distance. Took on her uncle's farm, who died suddenly.'

'That's she, back there upon the pony,' said Maryann.

Oak, his features smudged, grimy, and undiscoverable from the smoke and heat, his smock-frock burnt into holes and dripping with water, the ash stem of his sheep-crook charred six inches shorter, advanced with the humility stern adversity and thrust upon him up to the slight female form in the saddle. He lifted his hat with respect, and said in a hesitating voice, . . . 'Do you happen to want a shepherd, ma'am?'

She lifted the wool veil tied round her face, and looked all astonishment. Gabriel and his cold-hearted darling Bathsheba Everdene, were face to face.

CHAPTER SEVEN

RECOGNITION – A TIMID GIRL

Bathsheba withdrew into the shade. She scarcely knew whether most to be amused at the singularity of the meeting, or to be concerned at its awkwardness.

'Yes,' she murmured, 'I do want a shepherd. But—'

'He's the very man, ma'am,' said one of the villagers, quietly.

Conviction breed conviction. 'Ay, that 'a is,' said a second decisively.

'Then will you tell him to speak to the bailiff?' said Bathsheba.

All was practical again now. The bailiff pointed out to Gabriel, who, checking the palpitation within his breast retired with him to talk over the necessary preliminaries of hiring.

Bathsheba rode off into the darkness, and the men straggled on to the village in two and three—Oak and the bailiff being left by the rick alone.

'And now,' said the bailiff finally, 'all is settled about your coming, and I am going home-along. If you follow on the road till you come to Warren's Malthouse, where they are all gone, I dare say some of 'em will tell you of a place to stay. Goodnight to ye, shepherd.'

The bailiff went up the hill, and Oak walked on to the village, still astonished at the rencounter with Bathsheba, glad of his nearness to her, and perplexed at the rapidity with which the unpractised girl of Norcombe had developed into the supervising and cool woman here. But some women only require an emergency to make them fit for one.

Oak reached the churchyard, where several ancient trees grew. When abreast of a trunk which appeared to be the oldest of the old, he became aware that a figure was standing behind it.

It was a slim girl, rather thinly clad.

'Goodnight to you,' said Gabriel heartily.

'Goodnight,' said the girl to Gabriel.

The voice was unexpectedly attractive; it was the low and dulcet note suggestive of romance.

'I'll thank you to tell me if I'm in the way of Warren's Malthouse?' Gabriel resumed.

'Quite right. It's at the bottom of the hill. You are not a Weatherbury man?' she said timorously.

'I am not. I am the new shepherd—just arrived.'

'Only a shepherd—and you seem almost a farmer by your ways.'

'Only a shepherd.' Gabriel repeated with a dull cadence of finality. His thoughts were directed to the past, his eyes to the feet of the girl; and for the first time he saw lying there a bundle of some sort. She said coaxingly.—

'You won't say anything in the parish about having seen me here, will you—at least, not for a day or two?'

'I won't if you wish me not to,' said Oak.

'Thank you, indeed,' the other replied. 'I am rather poor, and I don't want people to know anything about me.' Then she was silent and shivered.

Gabriel said hesitatingly,—'Since you are not very well off, perhaps you would accept this trifle from me. It is only a shilling, but it is all I have to spare.'

'Yes, I will take it,' said the stranger gratefully.

She extended her hand; Gabriel his, Gabriel's fingers alighted on the young woman's wrists. It was beating with a throb of tragic intensity. It suggested a consumption too great of a vitality which, to judge from her figure and stature, was already too little.

'What is the matter?'

'Nothing. Let your having seen me be a secret!'

'Very well; I will. Goodnight, again.'

'Goodnight.'

The young girl remained motionless by the tree, and Gabriel descended into the village of Weatherbury.

CHAPTER EIGHT

THE MALTHOUSE – THE CHAT – NEWS

Warren's Malthouse was enclosed by an old wall inwrapped with ivy. There was no window in front; but a square hole in the door was glazed with a single pane. Voices were to be heard inside.

Oak's hand skimmed the surface of the door till he found a leather strap, which he pulled. This lifted a wooden latch, and the door swung open.

The room inside was lighted only by the ruddy glow from the kiln mouth, and in a remote corner was a small bed and bedstead, the owner and frequent occupier of which was the maltster.

This aged man was now sitting opposite the fire, his frosty white hair and beard overgrowing his gnarled figure.

Gabriel's nose was greeted by an atmosphere laden with the sweet smell of new malt. The conversation immediately ceased. Several exclaimed meditatively, 'Oh, 'tis the new shepherd, 'a b'lieve:'

'Come in, shepherd; sure ye be welcome, though we don't know yer name.'

'Gabriel Oak, that's my name, neighbours.'

'Come shepherd, and drink,' said the maltster. Gabriel took up the mug, drank an inch or more from the depth of its contents, and duly passed it to the next man.

'Drink, Henry Fray—drink,' magnanimously said Jan Coggan. Henry did not refuse. He was a man of more than middle age.

Mr Jan Coggan, who took the cup from Henry, was a crimson man with a spacious countenance and private glimmer in his eye.

'Why, Joseph Poorgrass, ye han't had a drop!' said Mr Coggan to a self-conscious man in the background, thrust the cup towards him.

'Such a modest man as he is!' said Jacob Smallbury. 'Why, ye've hardly had strength of eye enough to look in our young mis'ess's face, so I hear, Joseph?'

All looked at Joseph Poorgrass with pitying reproach.

'What sort of a place is this to live at, and what sort of a mis'ess is she to work under?' Gabriel's bosom thrilled gently as he thus slipped under the notice of the assembly the innermost subject of his heart.

'We d' know little of her—nothing. She only showed herself a few days ago. He uncle was took bad, and the doctor couldn't save the man. As I take it, she's going to keep on the farm.'

'And did any of you know Miss Everdene's father and mother?' inquired the shepherd.

'I knew them a little,' said Jacob Smallbury; 'but they were townsfolk, and didn't live here. They've been dead for years. Father, what sort of people were mis'ess' father and mother?'

'Well,' said the maltster, 'he wasn't much to look at; but she was a lovely woman. He was fond enough of her as his sweetheart.'

The end of Gabriel Oak's flute became visible over his smock-frock pocket, and Henry Fray exclaimed, 'Surely, shepherd, I seed you blowing into a great flute at Casterbridge?'

'You did,' said Gabriel, blushing faintly. 'I've been in great trouble, neighbours, and was driven to it. I used not to be so poor as I be now.'

'Never mind, heart!' said Mark Clark; 'You should take it careless-like, shepherd, and your time will come. But we could thank ye for a tune, if ye bain't too tired?'

Oak struck up 'Jockey to the Fair,' and played that sparkingly melody three times through in a most artistic and lively manner.

'He can blow the flute very well—that 'a can,' said a young married man, known as 'Susan Tall's husband.' He then wished them goodnight and withdrew.

Henry Fray was the first to follow. Then Gabriel arose and went off with Jan Coggan, who had offered him a lodging. A few minutes later, when the remaining ones were on their legs and about to depart, Fray came back again in a hurry.

'O—what's the matter, what's the matter, Henry?' said Joseph.

'The news is, that after Miss Everdene got home she went out again to see all was safe, as she usually do, and coming in found Baily Pennyways creeping down the granary steps with half a bushel of barley. She fleed at him like a cat and, to cut a long story short, he owned to having carried off five sack altogether, upon her promising not to persecute him. Well, he's turned out neck and crop, and my question is, who's going to be baily now?'

Before anyone could answer this profound question, in came the young man, Susan Tall's husband, in a still greater hurry.

'Have ye heard the news that's all over parish? Fanny Robin—Miss Everdene's youngest servant—can't be found. They've been wanting to lock up the door these two hours, but she isn't come in. They wouldn't be so concerned if she hadn't been noticed in such low spirits these last few days. . . . Well—Miss Everdene wants to speak to one or two of us before we go to bed.'

They all hastened up the lane to the farmhouse.

From the bedroom window above their heads Bathsheba's head and shoulders, robed in mystic white, were dimly seen extended into the air.

'Are any of my men among you?' she said anxiously.

'Yes ma'am, several,' said Susan Tall's husband.

'Tomorrow morning I wish two or three of you to make inquiries in the villages round if they have seen such a person as Fanny Robin. Do it quietly; there is no reason for alarm as yet.'

'I beg yer pardon, but had she any young man courting her in the parish, ma'am?' asked Jacob Smallbury.

'It is hardly likely, said Bathsheba. 'For any lover of hers might have come to the house if he had been a respectable lad.'

'She had no young man about here,' said a female voice from another window. 'Hers lives in Casterbridge, and I believe he's a soldier.'

'Do you know his name?' Bathsheba said.

'No, mistress; she was very close about it.'

'Perhaps I might be able to find out if I went to Casterbridge barracks,' said William Smallbury.

'Very well; if she doesn't return tomorrow, mind you go there and try to discover which man it is, and see him. I feel more responsible than I should if she had had any friends or relations alive. I do hope she has come to no harm through a man of that kind . . . . Do as I told you, then,' she said in conclusion, closing the casement.

'Ay ay, mistress; we will,' they replied, and moved away.

That night at Coggan's, Gabriel Oak, beneath the screen of closed eyelids, was busy with fancies. Night had always been the time at which he saw Bathsheba most vividly, and through the slow hours of shadow he tenderly regarded her image now. The delight of merely seeing her effaced for the time his perception of the great difference between seeing and possessing.

CHAPTER NINE

THE HOMESTEAD–A VISITOR –HALF-CONFIDENCES

By daylight, the bower of Oak's new-found mistress, Bathsheba Everdene, presented itself as a hoary building, of the early stage of Classic Renaissance as regards its architecture.

Lively voices were to be heard this morning in the upper rooms. In the room from which conversation proceeded Bathsheba and her servant-companion, Liddy Smallbury, were to be discovered sitting upon the floor, and sorting a complication of papers, books, bottles, and rubbish spread out thereon—remnants from the household stores of the late occupier. Liddy, the maltster's great-granddaughter, was about Bathsheba's equal in age, and her face was a prominent advertisement of the light-hearted English country girl.

Through a partly-opened door the noise of a scrubbing-brush led to the charwoman, Maryann Money.

'Stop your scrubbing a moment,' said Bathsheba through the door to her. 'I hear something.'

Maryann suspended the brush.

The tramp of a horse was apparent, approaching the front of the building. The paces slackened, turned in at the wicket, and, what was most unusual, came up the mossy path close to the door. The door was tapped with the end of a crop or stick.

The door opened, and a deep voice said—

'Is Miss Everdene at home?'

'I'll see, sir,' said Mrs Coggan, and in a minute appeared in the room. 'Here's Mr Boldwood wanting to see you, Miss Everdene.'

Bathsheba said at once—'I can't see him in this state. Whatever shall I do?'

Not-at-homes were hardly naturalized in Weatherbury farm-houses, so Liddy suggested—'Say you're a fright with dust, and can't come down.'

'Yes—that sounds very well,' said Mrs Coggan critically.

'Say I can't see him—that will do.'

Mrs Coggan went downstairs, and returned the answer.

'Oh, very well,' said the deep voice indifferently. 'All I wanted to ask was, if anything had been heard of Fanny Robin?'

'Nothing, sir—but we may know tonight. William Smallbury is gone to Casterbridge, where her young man lives, as is supposed, and the other men be inquiring about everywhere.'

The horse's tramp then recommenced and retreated, and the door closed.

'Who is Mr Boldwood?' said Bathsheba.

'A gentleman-farmer at Little Weatherbury.'

'Married?'

'No, miss.'

'How old is he?'

'Forty, I should say—very handsome—rather stern-looking—and rich.'

'Why should he inquire about Fanny?'

'Oh, because, as she had no friends in her childhood, he took her and put her to school, and got her place under your uncle. He's a very kind man that way but Lord, never was such a hopeless man for a woman! He's been courted by sixes and sevens—all the girls, gentle and simple, for miles round, have tried him!—Did anybody ever want to marry you miss?' Liddy ventured to ask. 'Lots of 'em I daresay?'

'A man wanted to once.'

'And you wouldn't have him?'

'He wasn't quite good enough for me.

'And did you love him, miss?'

'Oh no. But I rather liked him—Liddy, what footsteps are those I hear?'

Liddy looked from a back window into the courtyard behind. A crooked file of men was approaching the back door.

'The Philistines be upon us,' said Liddy, making her nose white against the glass.

'Oh, very well. Maryann, go down and keep them in the kitchen till I am dressed, and then show them in to me in the hall.'

CHAPTER TEN

MISTRESS AND MEN

Half-an-hour later Bathsheba, in finished dress, and followed by Liddy, entered the upper end of the old hall to find that her men had all deposited themselves on a long form and a settle at the lower extremity. She sat down at a table and opened the time-book, pen in her hand, with a canvas money-bag beside her. From this she poured a small heap of coin.

'Now, before I begin, men,' said Bathsheba, 'I have two matters to speak of. The first is that the bailiff is dismissed for thieving, and that I have formed a resolution to have no bailiff at all, but to manage everything with my own head and hands.'

The men breathed an audible breath of amazement.

'The next matter is, have you heard anything of Fanny?'

'I met Farmer Boldwood,' said Jacob Smallbury, 'and I went with him and two of his men, and dragged Newmill Pond, but we found nothing.

'And the new shepherd have been to Buck's Head, by Yalbury, thinking she had gone there, but nobody had seed her,' said Laban Tall.

'Hasn't William Smallbury been to Casterbridge?'

'Yes, ma'am, but he's not yet come home. He promised to be back by six.'

'It wants a quarter to six at present,' said Bathsheba looking at her watch. 'I daresay he'll be in directly. Well, now then,' she looked into the book—'Joseph Poorgrass, are you there?'

'Yes, sir—ma'am I mane,' said the person addressed. 'I be the personal name of Poorgrass.'

'How much to you?'

'Please nine and ninepence and a good halfpenny where 'twas a bad one, sir—ma'am I mane.'

'Quite correct. Now here are ten shillings in addition as a small present, as I am a new comer . . . how much do I owe you—that man in the corner—what's your name?'

'Matthew Moon, ma'am.'

'Matthew Moon,' murmured Bathsheba, turning her bright eyes to the book. 'Ten and twopence halfpenny is the sum put down to you, I see?'

'Yes, mis'ess,' said Matthew.

'Here it is, and ten shillings. Now the next—'

The names remaining were called in the same manner.

'Now I think I have done with you,' said Bathsheba, closing the book.

'The new shepherd will want a man under him,' suggested Henry Fray.

'Oh—he will. Who can he have?'

'Young Cainy Ball is a very good lad.' Henry said, 'and Shepherd Oak don't mind his youth?' he added, turning with an apologetic smile to the shepherd, who had just appeared on the scene.

'No, I don't mind that,' said Gabriel.

'Very well then, Cainy Ball to be under-shepherd.'

Footsteps were heard in the passage.

(All.) 'Here's Billy Smallbury come from Casterbridge.'

'Well, what about Fanny?' said Bathsheba, as William marched into the middle of the hall.

'Well, ma'am, in round numbers she's run away with the soldiers,' said William.

'No; not a steady girl like Fanny!'

'I'll tell ye the particulars. When I got to Casterbridge Barracks, they said, "The Eleventh Dragoon Guards be gone away, and new troops have come." '

Gabriel had listened with interest. 'I saw them go,' he said.

'And so I said to myself,' continued William, 'Fanny's young man was one of the regiment, and she's gone after him. There, ma'am, that's it in black and white.'

'Did you find out his name?'

'No; nobody knew it. I believe he was higher in rank than a private.'

Gabriel remained musing and said nothing, for he was in doubt.

'Well, we are not likely to know more tonight, at any rate,' said Bathsheba. 'But one of you had better run across to Farmer Boldwood's and tell him that much.'

She then rose, and surged out of the hall.

CHAPTER ELEVEN

FARMERS – A RULE – AN EXCEPTION

The first public evidence of Bathsheba's decision to be a farmer in her own person and by proxy no more was her appearance the following market-day in the cornmarket at Casterbridge.

The Corn Exchange was thronged with men who talked among each other in twos and threes. Among these heavy yeomen a feminine figure glided, the single one of her sex that the room contained. She was prettily and even daintily dressed. At her first entry the lumbering dialogues had ceased, nearly every face had been turned towards her, and those that were already turned rigidly fixed there.

The numerous evidences of her power to attract were only thrown into greater relief by a marked exception. Bathsheba, without looking within a right angle of him, was conscious of a black sheep among the flock. He was a gentlemanly man, with full and distinctly outlined Roman features. He was erect in attitude, and quiet in demeanour. One characteristic pre-eminently marked him—dignity.

Apparently he had some time ago reached that entrance to middle age at which a man's aspect naturally ceases to alter for the term of a dozen years or so; and, artificially, a woman's does likewise. Thirty-five and fifty were his limits of variation—he might have been either, or anywhere between the two.

Bathsheba was convinced that this unmoved person was not a married man.

When marketing was over, she rushed off to Liddy, who was waiting for her beside the yellow gig in which they had driven to town. The horse was put in, and on they trotted.

'I've been through it, Liddy, and it is over. I shan't mind it again, for they will all have grown accustomed to seeing me there; but this morning it was as bad as being married—eyes everywhere!'

'I knowed it would be,' Liddy said.

'But there was one man who had more sense than to waste his time upon me.' The information was put in this form that Liddy might not for a moment suppose her mistress was at all piqued. 'A very good-looking man,' she continued, 'upright; about forty, I should think. Do you know at all who he could be?'

Liddy couldn't think.

They bowled along in silence. A low carriage, bowling along still more rapidly behind a horse of unimpeachable breed, overtook and passed them.

'Why, there he is!' Bathsheba said.

Liddy looked. 'That! That's Farmer Boldwood—of course 'tis—the man you couldn't see the other day when he called.'

'Oh, Farmer Boldwood,' murmured Bathsheba. 'He's an interesting man,' she remarked.

CHAPTER TWELVE

THE VALENTINE

It was Sunday afternoon in the farmhouse, on the thirteenth of February. Dinner being over, Bathsheba, for want of a better companion, had asked Liddy to come and sit with her. Liddy, like a little brook, though shallow, was always rippling; her presence had not so much weight as to task thought, and yet enough to exercise it.

'Did you notice Mr Boldwood's doings in church this morning miss?' Liddy said.

'No, indeed,' said Bathsheba, with serene indifference.

'His pew is exactly opposite yours, miss, but he didn't turn his head to look at you once all the service.'

'Why should he?' again demanded her mistress, wearing a nettled look. 'I didn't ask him to.'

'Oh, no. But everybody else was noticing you; and it was odd he didn't. There, 'tis like him. Rich and gentlemanly, what does he care?'

Bathsheba dropped into a silence intended to express that she had opinions on the matter too abstruse for Liddy's comprehension.

'Dear me—I had nearly forgotten the valentine I bought yesterday,' she exclaimed at length.

'Valentine! Who for, miss?' said Liddy.

It is only for little Teddy Coggan. I have promised him something, and this will be a pretty surprise for him.'

Bathsheba took from her desk a gorgeously illuminated and embossed design, which had been bought on the previous market day. In the centre was a small oval enclosure; this was left blank.

'Here's a place for writing,' said Bathsheba. 'What shall I put?'

'Something of this sort, I should think,' returned Liddy promptly:—

'The rose is red
The violet blue
Carnation's sweet
And so are you.'

'Yes, that shall be it. It just suits itself to a chubby-faced child like him,' said Bathsheba. She inserted the words in a small though legible handwriting; enclosed the sheet in an envelope, and dipped her pen for the direction.

'What fun it would be to send it to the stupid old Boldwood, and how he would wonder!' said the irrepressible Liddy, lifting her eyebrows and indulging in an awful mirth.

Bathsheba paused to regard the idea at full length. Boldwood's had begun to be a troublesome image. It was faintly depressing that the most dignified and valuable man in the parish should withhold his eyes, and that a girl like Liddy should talk about it.

So Liddy's idea was at first rather harassing than piquant.

'No, I won't do that. He wouldn't see any humour in it.'

'He'd worry to death,' said the persistent Liddy.

'Let's toss, as men do,' said Bathsheba idly. 'Now then, head, Boldwood; tail, Teddy. No, we won't toss money on a Sunday, that would be tempting the devil indeed.'

'Toss this hymn-book; there can't be no sinfulness in that miss.'

'Very well. Open, Boldwood—shut, Teddy. No; it's more likely to fall open. Open, Teddy—shut, Boldwood.'

The book went fluttering in the air and came down shut.

Bathsheba, a small yawn upon her mouth, with off-hand serenity directed the missive to Boldwood.

'Now light a candle, Liddy. Which seal shall we use? Here's one with a motto—I remember it is some funny one, but I can't read it.'

A large red seal was duly affixed. Bathsheba looked closely at the hot wax to discover the words.

'Capital!' she exclaimed, throwing down the letter frolicsomely. ''Twould upset the solemnity of a person and clerk too.'

Liddy looked at the words of the seal and read—

'MARRY ME.'

CHAPTER THIRTEEN

EFFECT OF THE LETTER—SUNRISE

At dusk on the evening of St Valentine's Day Boldwood sat down to supper as usual, by a beaming fire of aged logs. Upon the mantelshelf before him was the letter Bathsheba had sent. Here the bachelor's gaze was continually fastening itself, till the large red seal became as a blot of blood on the retina of his eye; and as he ate and drank he still read in fancy the words thereon, although they were too remote for his sight—

'MARRY ME.'

Since the receipt of the missive in the morning. Boldwood had felt the symmetry of his existence to be slowly getting distorted in the direction of an ideal passion. When he went to bed he placed the valentine in the corner of the looking-glass. He was conscious of its presence, even when his back was turned upon it. It was the first time in Boldwood's life that such an event had occurred. The same fascination that caused him to think it an act which had a deliberate motive prevented him from regarding it as an impertinence. He looked again at the direction. Somebody's—some *woman's*—hand had travelled softly over the paper bearing his name; her brain had seen him in imagination the while. Why should she have imagined him? Her mouth—were the lips red and pale, plump or creased?—had curved itself to a certain expression as the pen went on—what had been the expression?

The vision of a woman writing, as a supplement to the words written, had no individuality. Whenever Boldwood dozed she took a form, and comparatively ceased to be a vision; when he awoke there was a letter justifying the dream.

The next morning, as the dawn drew on, Boldwood arose and dressed himself. He descended the stairs and went out towards the gate of a field to the east, leaning over which he paused and looked around. A half-muffled noise of light wheels interrupted him. Boldwood turned back into the road. It was the mail-cart. The driver held out a letter. Boldwood seized it and opened it, expecting another anonymous one.

'I don't think it is for you, sir,' said the man, when he saw Boldwood's action. 'Though there is no name, I think it is for your shepherd.'

Boldwood looked then at the address—

To the New Shepherd, Weatherbury Farm, New Casterbridge.

'Oh—what a mistake!' Boldwood said. It is not mine. Nor is it for my shepherd. It is for Miss Everdene's. I'll take it to him myself.'

CHAPTER FOURTEEN

A MORNING MEETING – THE LETTER AGAIN

The scarlet and orange light outside the malthouse did not penetrate to this interior, which was, as usual, lighted by a rival glow of similar hue, radiating from the hearth.

The maltster was breakfasting off bread and bacon. The form of Henry Fray advanced to the fire, stamping the snow from his boots when about halfway there.

Matthew Moon, Joseph Poorgrass, and other carters and waggoners followed at his heels.

'And how is she getting on without a baily?' the maltster inquired.

Henry shook his head, and smiled a bitter smile.

'She'll rue it—surely, surely!' he said. 'Benjy Pennyways were not a true man or an honest baily. But to think she can carr' on alone!' He allowed his head to swing laterally three or four times in silence.

A firm loud tread was now heard stamping outside; the door was opened about six inches, and somebody on the other side exclaimed—

'Neighbours, have ye got room for a few newborn lambs?'

'Ay, sure, shepherd,' said the conclave.

The door was flung back. Mr Oak appeared in the entry with a steaming face, looking altogether an epitome of the world's health and vigour. Four lambs hung in various embarrassing attitudes over his shoulders, and the dog George whom Gabriel had contrived to fetch from Norcombe, stalked solemnly behind.

Oak lowered the lambs from their unnatural elevation, wrapped them in hay, and placed them round the fire.

'We've no lambing-hut here, as I used to have at Norcombe,' said Gabriel, 'and 'tis such a plague to bring the weakly ones to a house. If 'twasn't for your place here maltster, I don't know what I should do, this keen weather.'

The genial warmth of the fire now began to stimulate the nearly lifeless lambs to bleat and move their limbs briskly, and to recognise for the first time the fact that they were born. Oak pulled the milk-can from before the fore, and taking a small tea-pot from the pocket of his smock-frock, filled it with milk, and taught those of the helpless creatures which were not to be restored to their dams to drinks from the spout—a trick they acquired with astonishing aptitude.

A shade darkened the door, and Boldwood entered the malthouse, bestowing upon each a nod of a quality between friendliness and condescension.

'Ah! Oak, I thought you were here,' he said, 'I met the mailcart ten minutes ago, and a letter was put into my hand, which I opened without reading the address. I believe it is yours. You must excuse the accident, please.'

'O yes—not a bit of difference, Mr Boldwood—not a bit,' said Gabriel readily. He stepped aside, and read the following in an unknown hand:—

'DEAR FRIEND – I do not know your name, but I think these few lines will reach you, which I write to thank you for your kindness to me the night I left Weatherbury in a reckless way. I also return the money I owe you. All has ended well, and I am happy to say I am going to be married to the young man who has courted me for some time—Sergeant Troy, of the 11th Dragoon Guards, now quartered in this town, a man of great respectability and high honour—indeed a nobleman by blood.

'I should be much obliged to you if you would keep the contents of this letter a secret for the present, dear friend. We mean to surprise Weatherbury by coming there soon as husband and wife, though I blush to state it to one nearly a stranger. The sergeant grew up in Weatherbury. Thanking you again for your kindness.

I am, your sincere will-wisher,

FANNY ROBIN.'

'Have you read it, Mr Boldwood? said Gabriel; 'if not, you had better do so. I know you are interested in Fanny Robin.'

Boldwood read the letter and looked grieved.

'Fanny—poor Fanny! the end she is so confident of has not yet come and may never come. I see she gives no address.'

'What sort of a man is this Sergeant Troy?' said Gabriel.

'H'm—I'm afraid not one to build much hope upon in such a case as this,' the farmer murmured, 'though he's a clever fellow, and up to everything. A slight romance attaches to him, too. His mother was a French governess, and it seems that a secret attachment existed between her and the late Lord Severn. She was married to a poor medical man, and soon after an infant was born; and while money was forthcoming all went on well.

Unfortunately for her boy, his best friends died; and he got then a situation as second clerk at a lawyer's in Casterbridge. He stayed there for some time, and might have worked himself into a dignified position of some sort had he not indulged in the wild freak of enlisting. I have much doubt if ever little Fanny will surprise us in the way she mentions—very much doubt. A silly girl—silly girl!'

The farmer drew out his pocket-book, unfastened it, and allowed it to lie open on his hand. A letter was revealed—Bathsheba's.

'I was going to ask you, Oak,' he said, with unreal carelessness, 'if you know whose writing this is?'

Oak glanced into the book, and replied instantly, with a flushed face, 'Miss Everdene's.'

Oak had coloured simply at the consciousness of sounding her name. He now felt a strangely distressing qualm from a new thought. The letter could of course be no other than anonymous, or the inquiry would not have been necessary.

Soon parting from Gabriel, the lonely and reserved man returned to his house to breakfast. He again placed the letter on the mantelpiece, and sat down to think of the circumstances attending it by the light of Gabriel's information.

CHAPTER FIFTEEN

ALL SAINTS' AND ALL SOULS'

On a week-day morning a small congregation, consisting mainly of women and girls, rose from its knees in the mouldy nave of a church called All Saints', in a distant barrack-town. They were about to disperse, when a smart footstep, entering a porch and coming up the central passage, arrested their attention. A young cavalry soldier in a red uniform, with the three chevrons of a sergeant upon his sleeve, strode up the aisle, with an embarrassment which was only the more marked by the intense vigour of his step, and by the determination upon his face to show none. He never paused till he came close to the altar railing. Here for a moment he stood alone.

The officiating curate, who had not yet doffed his surplice, perceived the new-comer, and followed him to the communion-space. He whispered to the soldier, and then beckoned to the clerk, who in his turn whispered to an elderly woman, apparently his wife, and they also went up the chancel steps.

' 'Tis a wedding!' murmured some of the women, brightening 'Let's wait!'

The majority again sat down.

The jack had struck half-past eleven.

'Where's the woman?' whispered some of the spectators.

The young sergeant stood still with the abnormal rigidity of the old pillars around. He faced the south-east, and was as silent as he was still.

The silence grew to be a noticeable thing as the minutes went on, and nobody else appeared, and not a soul moved. The rattle of the quarter-jack, its blows for three-quarters, were almost painfully abrupt, and caused many of the congregation to start palpably.

There began now that slight shifting of feet, that artificial coughing which betrays a nervous suspense. At length there was a titter. But the soldier never moved. There he stood his face to the south-east, upright as a column, his cap in his hand.

The clock ticked on. The women threw off their nervousness, and titters and giggling became more frequent. Then followed the dull and remote resonance of the twelve heavy strokes in the tower above. The women were impressed, and there was no giggle this time.

The clergyman glided into the vestry, and the clerk vanished.

The sergeant had not yet turned; every woman in the church was waiting to see his face, and he appeared to know it. At last he did turn, and stalked resolutely down the nave, braving them all, with a compressed lip.

Opposite to the church was a paved square. The young man on leaving the door went to cross the square, when, in the middle he met a little woman. The expression of her face, which had been one of intense anxiety, sank at the sight of his nearly to terror.

'Well?' he said, in a suppressed passion, fixedly looking at her.

'O Frank—I made a mistake!—I thought that church with the spire was All Saints', and I was at the door at half-past eleven to a minute as you said. I waited till a quarter to twelve, and found then that I was in All Souls'. But I wasn't much frightened, for I thought it could be tomorrow as well.'

'Tomorrow! And he gave vent to a hoarse laugh. 'I don't go through that experience again for some time, I warrant you!'

'But after all,' she expostulated in a trembling voice, 'the mistake was not such a terrible thing! Now, dear Frank, when shall it be?'

'Ah, when? God knows!' he said, with a light irony, and turning from her walked rapidly away.

CHAPTER SIXTEEN

BOLDWOOD IN MEDITATION—REGRET

On Saturday Boldwood was in Casterbridge market-house as usual, when the disturber of his dreams entered, and became visible to him.

Boldwood looked at her, not silly, critically or understandingly, but blankly. He saw her black hair, the correct facial curves and profile, and the roundness of her chin and throat. He saw then the side of her eyelids, eyes and lashes, and the shape of her ear. Next he noticed her figure, her skirt, and the very soles of her shoes.

Boldwood thought her beautiful, but wondered whether he was right in his thought. He furtively said to a neighbour. 'Is Miss Everdene considered handsome?'

'Oh yes! A very handsome girl indeed.'

A man is never more credulous than in receiving favourable opinions on the beauty of a woman he is half, or quite, in love with. Boldwood was satisfied now.

Boldwood was tenant of what was called Little Weatherbury Farm, and his person was the nearest approach to aristocracy that this remoter quarter of the parish could boast of.

His house stood recessed from the road, and the stables, which are to a farm what a fireplace is to a room, were behind. Inside the blue door were to be seen at this time the backs and tails of half-a-dozen warm and contented horses standing in their stalls.

Pacing up and down at the heels of the animals was Farmer Boldwood himself. His square-framed perpendicularity showed fully and his fine reddish-fleshed face was bent downwards just enough to render obscure the still mouth and the well-rounded though rather prominent and broad chin. A few clear and thread-like horizontal lines were the only interruption to the otherwise smooth surface of his large forehead.

The phases of Boldwood's life were ordinary enough, but his was not an ordinary nature. His equilibrium disturbed, he was in extremity at once. If an emotion possessed him at all, it ruled him; a feeling not mastering him was entirely latent. Stagnant or rapid, it was never slow. He was always hit mortally, or he was missed.

He had no light and careless touches in his constitution either for good or for evil. Stern in the outlines of action, mild in the details, he was serious thoughout all. Had Bathsheba known Boldwood's moods her blame would have been fearful, and the stain upon her heart ineradicable. Moreover, had she known her present power for good or evil over this man, she would have trembled at her responsibility. Luckily for her present, unluckily for her future tranquillity, her understanding had not yet told her what Boldwood was.

Farmer Boldwood came to the stable-door and looked forth across the level fields to a meadow belonging to Bathsheba's farm.

Boldwood saw there three figures. They were those of Miss Everdene, Shepherd Oak, and Cainy Ball.

When Bathsheba's figure shone upon the farmer's eyes it lighted him up as the moon lights up a great tower. There was a change in Boldwood's exterior from its former impassibleness; and his face showed that he was now living outside his defences for the first time, and with a fearful sense of exposure. It is the usual experience of strong natures when they love.

At last he arrived at a conclusion. It was to go across and inquire boldly of her.

He approached the gate of the meadow. Mistress and man were engaged in the operation of making a lamb 'take', which is performed whenever an ewe has lost her own offspring, one of the twins of another ewe being given her as a substitute.

Gabriel had skinned the dead lamb, and was tying the skin over the body of the live lamb in the customary manner, whilst Bathsheba was holding open a little pen of four hurdles into which the mother and foisted lamb were driven, where they would remain till the old sheep conceived an affection for the young one.

Bathsheba looked up and saw the farmer by the gate. Gabriel to whom her face was as the uncertain glory of an April day, instantly discerned thereon the mark of some influence from without, in the form of a keenly self-conscious reddening. He also turned and beheld Boldwood.

Farmer Boldwood had read the pantomine denoting that they were aware of his presence, and the presence, and the perception was as too much light turned upon his new sensibility. He was still in the road, and by moving on he hoped that neither would recognize that he had originally intended to enter the field. He passed by with an utter and overwhelming sensation of ignorance, shyness, and doubt. Perhaps in her manner there were signs that she wished to see him—perhaps not—he could not read a woman.

As for Bathsheba, she was not deceived into the belief that Farmer Boldwood had walked by on business or in idleness. She concluded that she was herself responsible for Boldwood's appearance there. It troubled her much to see what a great flame a little wildfire was likely to kindle. Bathsheba was no schemer for marriage, nor was she deliberately a trifler with the affections of men.

She resolved never again, by look or by sign, to interrupt the steady flow of this man's life. But a resolution to avoid an evil is seldom framed till the evil is so far advanced as to make avoidance impossible.

CHAPTER SEVENTEEN

THE SHEEP-WASHING—THE OFFER

Boldwood did eventually call upon her.

It was the end of May and he had by this time grown used to being in love; the passion now startled him less even when it tortured him more, and he felt himself adequate to the situation. On inquiring for her at her house they had told him she was at the sheep-washing, and he went off to seek her there.

The sheep-washing pool was a perfectly circular basin of brick-work in the meadows, full of the clearest water. Shepherd Oak, Jan Coggan, Moon, Poorgrass, Cain Ball, and several others were assembled here, all dripping wet to the very roots of their hair, and Bathsheba was standing by in a new riding-habit—the most elegant she had ever worn—the reins of her horse being looped over her arm.

Flagons of cider were rolling about upon the green. The meek sheep were pushed into the pool by Coggan and Matthew Moon, who stood by the lower hatch, immersed to their waists; then Gabriel, who stood on the brink, thrust them under as they swam along with an instrument like a crutch, formed for the purpose, and also for assisting the exhausted animals when the wool became saturated and they began to sink. They were let out against the stream, and through the upper opening, all impurities flowing away below. Cainy Ball and Joseph, who performed this latter operation, were if possible wetter than the rest.

Boldwood came close and bade her good morning with such constraint that she could not but think he had stepped across to the washing for its own sake, hoping not to find her there; more, she fancied his brow severe and his eye slighting. Bathsheba immediately contrived to withdraw, and glided along by the river till she was completely past its bend. She heard footsteps brushing the grass, and had a consciousness that love was encircling her like a perfume.

'Miss Everdene!' said the farmer.

She trembled, turned, and said 'Good morning.' His tone was so utterly removed from all she had expected as a beginning. It was lowness and quiet accentuated: an emphasis of deep meanings, their form, at the same time, being scarcely expressed.

'I feel—almost too much—to think,' he said, with a solemn simplicity. 'I have come to speak to you without preface—I come to make you an offer of marriage.'

Bathsheba tried to preserve an absolutely neutral countenance.

'I am now forty-one years old,' he went on. 'I may have been called a confirmed bachelor, and I was a confirmed bachelor. But we all change, and my change, in this matter, came with seeing you. Beyond all things, I want you as my wife. My life is a burden without you. I want you to let me say I love you again and again!'

'Mr Boldwood, it is painful to have to say I am surprised, so that I don't know how to answer you with propriety and respect—but am only just able to speak out my feeling—I mean my meaning; that I am afraid I can't marry you, much as I respect you. You are too dignified for me to suit you, sir.'

'I wish I could say courteous flatteries to you,' the farmer continued, 'and put my rugged feeling into a graceful shape: but I have neither power nor patience to learn such things. I want you for my wife—so wildly that no other feeling can abide in me; but I should not have spoken out had I not been led to hope.'

'I—I didn't—I know I ought never to have dreamt of sending that valentine—forgive me, sir—it was a wanton thing which no woman with any self-respect should have done. If you will only pardon my thoughtlessness, I promise never to—'

'No, no, no. Don't say thoughtlessness! Make me think it was something more—that it was a sort of prophetic instinct—the beginning of a feeling that you would like me. You torture me to say it was done in thoughtlessness—I never thought of it in that light, and I can't endure it. Ah! I wish I knew how to win you! I cannot say how far above every other idea and object on earth you seem to me—nobody knows—God only knows—how much you are to me!'

Bathsheba's heart was young, and it swelled with sympathy for the deep-natured man who spoke so simply.

'Don't say it: don't! I cannot bear you to feel so much, and me to feel nothing. And I am afraid they will notice us, Mr Boldwood. Will you let the matter rest now?'

'Say then, that you don't absolutely refuse. Do not quite refuse?'

'I can do nothing. I cannot answer.'

'I will call upon you again tomorrow.'

'No—please not. Give me time.'

'I will give you any time,' he said earnestly and gratefully.

And then she turned away. Boldwood dropped his gaze to the ground, and stood long like a man who did not know where he was.

CHAPTER EIGHTEEN

THE GREAT BARN AND THE SHEEP-SHEARERS

It was the first day of June, and the sheep-shearing season culminated, the landscape, even to the leanest pasture, being all health and colour. Gold was palpably present in the country, and the devil had gone with the world to town. In the metamorphosed figures of Mr Jan Coggan, the master-shearer, Henry Fray, Susan Tall's husband, Joseph Poorgrass, young Cain Ball as assistant-shearer, and Gabriel Oak as general supervisor, a fixity of facial machinery in general proclaimed that serious work was the order of the day.

They sheared in the great barn. Here the shearers knelt, the sun slanting in upon their bleached shirts, tanned arms, and the polished shears they flourished, causing these to bristle with a thousand rays strong enough to blind a weak-eyed man. The sheep being all collected in a crowd, in one angle a catching-pen was formed, in which three or four sheep were continuously kept ready for the shearers to seize without loss of time. In the background were three women gathering up the fleeces.

Behind all was Bathsheba, carefully watching the men to see that there was no cutting or wounding through carelessness, and that the animals were shorn close. Gabriel, who flitted and hovered under her bright eyes like a moth, did not shear continuously, half his time being spent in attending to the others and selecting the sheep for them.

Bathsheba came to Gabriel as he dragged a frightened ewe to his shear-station, flinging it over upon its back with a dexterous twist of the arm. He lopped off the tresses about its head, and opened up the neck and collar, his mistress quietly looking on.

Poor Gabriel's soul was fed with a luxury of content by having her over him, her eyes critically regarding his skilful shears, which apparently were going to gather up a piece of the flesh at every close, and yet never did so.

'Well done, and done quickly!' said Bathsheba, looking at her watch as the last snip resounded and the clean, sleek creature arose from its fleece.

'How long, miss?' said Gabriel, wiping his brow.

'Three-and-twenty minutes and a half since you took the first lock from its forehead. It is the first time that I have ever seen one done in less than half an hour.'

But heartless circumstance could not leave entire Gabriel's happiness of this morning. Oak's belief that she was going to stand pleasantly by and time him through another performance was painfully interrupted by Farmer Boldwood's appearance in the extremest corner of the barn. Nobody seemed to have perceived his entry, but there he certainly was.

He crossed over towards Bathsheba, who turned to greet him with a carriage of perfect ease. He spoke to her in low tones; and she instinctively modulated her own to the same pitch, and her voice ultimately even caught the inflection of his. The issue of their dialogue was the taking of her hand by the courteous farmer to help her into the bright June sunlight outside. Gabriel sheared on, constrained and sad.

She left Boldwood's side, and he walked up and down alone for nearly a quarter of an hour. Then she reappeared in her new riding-habit of myrtle-green, and young Bob Coggan led on her mare, Boldwood fetching his own horse from the tree under which it had been tied.

Boldwood gently tossed Bathsheba into the saddle. The horses' heads were put about, and they trotted away.

'That means matrimony,' said Temperance Miller, following them out of sight with her eyes.

'I reckon that's the size o't,' said Coggan, working along without looking up.

Oak went on with his shearing, and said not a word. He was inwardly convinced that that day would see Boldwood the accepted husband of Miss Everdene. He adored Bathsheba just the same.

CHAPTER NINETEEN

EVENTIDE—A SECOND DECLARATION

For the shearing-supper a long table was placed on the grass-plot beside the house, the end of the table being thrust over the sill of the wide parlour window and a foot or two into the room. Miss Everdene sat inside the window, facing down the table. She was thus at the head without mingling with the men.

This evening Bathsheba was unusually excited, her red cheeks and lips contrasting lustrously with her shadowy hair. She seemed to expect assistance, and the seat at the bottom of the table was at her request left vacant. Mr Boldwood came in at the gate, and crossed the green to Bathsheba at the window. He apologized for his lateness; his arrival was evidently by arrangement.

The gentleman-farmer was dressed in cheerful style, in a new coat and a white waistcoat, quite contrasting with his usual sober suits of grey. Inwardly, too, he was blithe, and consequently chatty to an exceptional degree. So also was Bathsheba now that he had come.

The sun went down in an ochreous mist; supper being ended, the men talked on and grew merry. Bathsheba still remained enthroned inside the window, and occupied herself in knitting. Boldwood had gone inside the room, and was sitting near her.

Next came the question of the evening. Would Miss Everdene sing to them the song she always sang so charmingly—'The Banks of Allan Water'—before they went home?

After a moment's consideration Bathsheba assented, beckoning to Gabriel, who hastened up into the coveted atmosphere.

'Have you brought your flute?' she whispered.

'Yes miss.'

'Play to my singing then.'

Her singing was soft and rather tremulous at first, but it soon swelled to a steady clearness. Subsequent events caused one of the verses to be remembered for many months, and even years, by more than one of those who were gathered there:—

For his bride a soldier sought her.
And a winning tongue had he;
On the banks of Allan Water
None was gay as she!

The shearers reclined against each other and so silent and absorbed were they that her breathing could almost be heard between the bars; and at the end of the ballad, when the last tone loitered on to an inexpressible close, there arose that buzz of pleasure which is the attar of applause.

Bathsheba then wished them goodnight, withdrew from the window, and retired to the back part of the room, Boldwood thereupon closing the sash and the shutters, and remaining inside with her. Oak wandered away under the quiet and scented trees. Recovering from the softer impressions produced by Bathsheba's voice, the shearers rose to leave.

At this time of departure a passionate scene was in course of enactment in the parlour. Miss Everdene and Boldwood were alone.

She was standing behind a low armchair, from which she had just risen, and he was kneeling in it—inclining himself over its back towards her, and holding her hand in both his own.

'I will try to love you,' she was saying, in a trembling voice quite unlike her usual self-confidence. 'And if I can believe in any way that I shall make you a good wife I shall indeed be willing to marry you. But, Mr Boldwood, hesitation on so high a matter is honourable in any woman, and I don't want to give a solemn promise tonight. I would rather ask you to wait a few weeks till I can see my situation better.'

'But you have every reason to believe that *then*—'

'I have every reason to hope that at the end of the five or six weeks, between this time and harvest, that you say you are going to be away from home, I shall be able to promise to be your wife,' she said firmly. 'But remember this distinctly, I don't promise yet.'

'It is enough; I don't ask more. I can wait on those dear words. And now, Miss Everdene, goodnight!'

Goodnight, she said graciously—almost tenderly; and Boldwood withdrew with a serene smile.

CHAPTER TWENTY

THE SAME NIGHT—THE FIR PLANTATION

Among the multifarious duties which Bathsheba had voluntarily imposed upon herself by dispensing with the services of a bailiff, was the particular one of looking round the homestead before going to bed, to see that all was right and safe for the night.

Her way back to the house was by a path through a young plantation of tapering firs, which had been planted some years earlier to shelter the premises from the north wind. By reason of the density of the foliage overhead it was dark as midnight there at dusk. Slipping along here on her way home this night, Bathsheba fancied she could hear footsteps entering the track at the opposite end. The noise approached, came close, and a figure was apparently on the point of gliding past her when something tugged at her skirt and pinned it forcibly to the ground. The instantaneous check nearly threw Bathsheba off her balance. In recovering she struck against warm clothes and buttons.

'A rum start, upon my soul!' said a masculine voice, a foot or so above her head. 'Have I hurt you, mate?'

'No,' said Bathsheba, attempting to shrink away.

'Are you a woman?'

'Yes.'

'A lady, I should have said.'

Bathsheba softly tugged again, but to no purpose.

'Is that a dark lantern you have? I fancy so,' said the man.

'If you'll allow me I'll open it, and set you free.'

A hand seized the lantern, the door was opened, the rays burst out from their prison, and Bathsheba beheld her position with astonishment.

The man to whom she was hooked was brilliant in brass and scarlet. He was a soldier. His sudden appearance was to darkness what the sound of a trumpet is to silence. The contrast of this revelation with her anticipations of some sinister figure was so great that it had upon her the effect of a fairy transformation.

It was immediately apparent that the military man's spur had become entangled in the gimp which decorated the skirt of her dress. He caught a view of her face.

He looked hard into her eyes when she raised them for a moment; Bathsheba looked down again, for his gaze was too strong to be received point-blank with her own. But she had obliquely noticed that he was young and slim, and that he wore three chevrons upon his sleeve.

Bathsheba pulled again.

'You are a prisoner, miss; it is no use blinking the matter,' said the soldier drily. 'I must cut your dress if you are in such a hurry.'

'Yes—please do!' she exclaimed helplessly.

'It wouldn't be necessary if you could wait a moment'; and he unwound a cord from the little wheel.

His unravelling went on, but it nevertheless seemed coming to no end. She looked at him again. 'Thank you for the sight of such a beautiful face!' said the young sergeant, without ceremony.

'Go on your way, please.'

'What, Beauty, and drag you after me? Do but look; I never saw such a tangle!'

'O, 'tis shameful of you; you have been making it worse on purpose to keep me here—you have!'

'Indeed, I don't think so,' said the sergeant, with a merry twinkle.

'I tell you you have!' she exclaimed, in high temper, 'I insist upon undoing it. Now, allow me!'

'Certainly miss; I am not of steel.' He added a sigh which had as much archness in it as a sigh could possess without losing its nature altogether.

'I've seen a good many women in my time,' he continued in a murmur, 'but I've never seen a woman so beautiful as you. Take it or leave it—be offended or like it—I don't care.'

'Who are you, then, who can so well afford to despise opinion?'

'No stranger. Sergeant Troy. I am staying in this place.—There it is undone at last you see. Your light fingers were more eager than mine.'

She started up, and so did he. How to decently get away from him—that was her difficulty now. She sidled off inch by inch, the lantern in her hand, till she could see the redness of his coat no longer.

'Ah, Beauty; goodbye!' he cried.

She made no reply, and, reaching a distance of twenty or thirty yards, turned about, and ran indoors.

Liddy had just retired to rest. In ascending to her own chamber, Bathsheba opened the girl's door an inch or two, and, panting, said—

'Liddy, is any soldier staying in the village—sergeant somebody—rather gentlemanly for a sergeant, and good looking—a red coat with blue facings?'

'No miss. . . . No, I say; but really it might be Sergeant Troy home on furlough, though I have not seen him. He was here once in that way when the regiment was at Casterbridge.'

'What kind of a person is he?'

'O! miss—I blush to name it—a gay man! But I know him to be very quick and trim, who might have made his thousands, like a squire. He's a doctor's son by name, which is a great deal; and he's an earl's son by nature!'

'Which is a great deal more. Goodnight, Liddy.

After all, how could a cheerful wearer of skirts be permanently offended with the man? There are occasions when girls like Bathsheba will put up with a great deal of unconventional behaviour. When they want to be praised, which is often; when they want to be mastered, which is sometimes; and when they want no nonsense, which is seldom. Just now the first feeling was in the ascendant with Bathsheba, with a dash of the second.

It was a fatal omission of Boldwood's that he had never once told her she was beautiful.

CHAPTER TWENTY-ONE

THE NEW ACQUAINTANCE DESCRIBED —A SECOND MEETING

Idiosyncrasy and vicissitude had combined to stamp Sergeant Troy as an exceptional being.

He was a man to whom memories were an incumbrance, and anticipations a superfluity. Simply feeling, considering, and caring for what was before his eyes, he was vulnerable only in the present. With him the past was yesterday; the future, tomorrow; never, the day after.

Sergeant Troy, being entirely innocent of the practice of expectation, was never disappointed. To set against this negative gain there may have been some positive losses from a certain narrowing of the higher tastes and sensations which it entailed. But what Troy had never enjoyed he did not miss; but being fully conscious that what sober people missed he enjoyed, his capacity, though really less, seemed greater than theirs.

He was moderately truthful towards men, but to women lied unashamedly—a system of ethics above all others calculated to win popularity at the first flush of admission into lively society; and the possibility of favour gained being transitory had reference *only* to the future.

He never passed the line which divides the spruce vices from the ugly; and hence, though his morals had hardly been applauded, disapproval of them had frequently been tempered with a smile.

He was a fairly well-educated man for one of middle class–exceptionally well educated for a common soldier. He spoke fluently and unceasingly. He could in this way be one thing and seem another; for instance, he could speak of love and think of dinner; call on the husband to look at the wife; be eager to pay and intend to owe.

He had been known to observe casually that in dealing with womankind the only alternative to flattery was cursing and swearing. There was no third method. 'Treat them fairly, and you are a lost man,' he would say.

A week or two after the shearing Bathsheba approached her hayfields and looked over the hedge towards the haymakers. In the first mead they were already loading hay, the women raking it into cocks and windrows, and the men tossing it upon the waggon.

From behind the waggon a bright scarlet spot emerged, and went on loading unconcernedly with the rest. It was the gallant sergeant, who had come haymaking for pleasure; and nobody could deny that he was doing the mistress of the farm real knight-service by this voluntary contribution of his labour at a busy time.

As soon as Bathsheba had entered the field Troy saw her and came forward. 'Ah Miss Everdene!' he said, touching his dimunitive cap. 'Little did I think it was you I was speaking to the other night. I step across now to beg your forgiveness a thousand times for having been led by my feelings to express myself too strongly for a stranger. To be sure I am no stranger—I am Sergeant Troy, as I told you, and I have assisted your uncle in this fields no end of times when I was a lad. I have been doing the same for you today.'

'I thank you for giving help here,' Bathsheba said. 'But mind you don't speak to me again unless I speak to you.'

'O Miss Bathsheba! That is too hard! You will never speak to me for I shall not be here long. Well, perhaps generosity is not a woman's most marked characteristic.'

'But you can't really care for a word for me? Why, you only saw me the other night!'

'That makes no difference. The lightning works instantaneously. I loved you then at once—as I do now.'

'You cannot and you don't. There is no such sudden feeling in people. I won't listen to you any longer. I am going—'

'But will you speak to me for these few weeks of my stay?'

'Yes, I suppose so; if it is any pleasure to you.'

'Miss Everdene. I thank you.'

Bathsheba withdrew, her heart erratically flitting hither and thither from perplexed excitement. She retreated homeward murmuring, 'O what does it mean! I wish I knew how much of it was true!'

CHAPTER TWENTY-TWO

HIVING THE BEES

The Weatherbury bees were late in their swarming this year. It was the latter part of June, and the day after the interview with Troy in the hayfield, that Bathsheba was standing in her garden, watching a swarm in the air and guessing their probable settling place.

The men and women being all busily engaged in saving the hay, Bathsheba resolved to hive the bees herself, if possible. She had dressed the hive with herbs and honey, fetched a ladder, brush, and crook, made herself impregnable with armour of leather gloves, straw hat, and large gauze veil, and ascended a dozen rungs of the ladder. At once she heard not ten yards off, a voice that was beginning to have a strange power in agitating her.

'Miss Everdene, let me assist you; you should not attempt such a thing alone.'

Troy was just opening the garden gate.

Bathsheba flung down the brush, crook, and empty hive in a tremendous flurry, and as well as she could slid down the ladder.

By the time she reached the bottom Troy was there also, and he stooped to pick up the hive.

'How fortunate I am to have dropped in at this moment!' exclaimed the sergeant.

She found her voice in a minute. 'What! and will you shake them in for me?' she asked.

'Will I!' said Troy. 'Why of course I will,' Troy flung down his cane and put his foot on the ladder to ascend.

'But you must have on the veil and gloves, or you'll be stung fearfully! And you must have the broad-brimmed hat, too; for your cap has no brim to keep the veil off, and they'd reach your face.'

So a whimsical fate ordered that her hat should be taken off—veil and all attached—and placed upon his head, and the gloves put on him.

Bathsheba looked on from the ground whilst he was busy sweeping and shaking the bees from the tree, holding up the hive with the other hand for them to fall into.

'Upon my life,' said Troy, through the veil, 'holding up this hive makes one's arm ache worse than a week of sword-exercise.' When the manoeuvre was complete he approached her. 'Would you be good enough to untie me and let me out? I am nearly stifled inside the silk cage.'

To hide her embarrassment during the unwonted process of untying the string about his neck, she said:—

'I have never seen that you spoke of.'

'What?'

'The sword-exercise.'

'Ah! Would you like to?' said Troy.

Bathsheba hesitated. She had heard wondrous reports of this strange and glorious performance, the sword-exercise. She said mildly what she felt strongly:

'Yes; I should like to see it very much.'

'And so you shall; you shall see me go through it. I have no sword here; but I think I could get one by the evening. Now, will you do this?'

Troy bent over her and murmured some suggestion in a low voice.

'O no, indeed; I couldn't,' said Bathsheba, blushing.

'Surely you might? Nobody would know.'

Bathsheba hesitated. 'Well, I'll come. But only for a very short time,' she added: 'a very short time.'

'It will not take five minutes,' said Troy.

CHAPTER TWENTY-THREE

THE HOLLOW AMID THE FERNS

The hill opposite Bathsheba's dwelling extended, a mile off, into an uncultivated tract of land, dotted at this season with tall thickets of brake fern. The bristling ball of gold in the west still swept the ferns with its rays when Bathsheba appeared in their midst, their soft, feathery arms caressing her up to her shoulders. She reached the verge of a pit in the middle of the ferns. Troy stood in the bottom, looking up towards her.

'I heard you rustling through the fern before I saw you,' he said, coming up and giving her his hand to help her down the slope.

'Now,' said Troy, producing the sword, which as he raised it into the sunlight, gleamed a sort of greeting, like a living thing. 'You are my antagonist, with this difference from real warfare, that I shall miss you every time by one hair's breadth, or perhaps two. Mind you don't flinch, whatever you do.'

'I'll be sure not to!' she said invincibly.

He pointed to about a yard in front of him.

Bathsheba's adventurous spirit was beginning to find some grains of relish in these highly novel proceedings. She took up her position as directed, facing Troy.

'Is the sword very sharp?'

'O no—only stand as still as a statue. Now!'

In an instant the atmosphere was transformed to Bathsheba's eyes. Beams of light caught from the low sun's rays, above, around, in front of her, well-nigh shut out earth and heaven—around, in front of her, well-nigh shut out earth and heaven—all emitted in the marvellous evolutions of Troy's reflecting blade, which seemed everywhere at once, and yet nowhere specially.

Never since the broadsword became the national weapon had there been more dexterity shown in its management than by the hands of Sergeant Troy, and never had he been in such splendid temper for the performance as now in the evening sunshine among the ferns with Bathsheba. It may safely be asserted with respect to the closeness of his cuts, that had it been possible for the edge of the sword to leave in the air a permanent substance whenever it flew past, the space left untouched would have been almost a mould of Bathsheba's figure.

She could see the hue of Troy's sword arm, spread in a scarlet haze over the space covered by its motions, and behind all Troy himself, his eye always keenly measuring her breadth and outline, and his lips tightly closed in sustained effort. Next, his movements lapsed slower, and she could see them individually. The hissing of the sword had ceased, and he stopped entirely.

'The outer loose lock of hair wants tidying,' he said, before she had moved or spoken. 'Wait: I'll do it for you.'

An arc of silver shone on her right side: the sword had descended. The lock dropped to the ground.

'Bravely borne!' said Troy. 'You didn't flinch a shade's thickness. Wonderful in a woman!'

'But how could you chop off a curl of my hair with a sword that has no edge?'

'No edge! This sword will shave like a razor!'

'But you said before beginning that it was blunt and couldn't cut me!'

'That was to get you to stand still, and so make sure of your safety. The risk of injuring you through your moving was too great not to force me to tell you a fib to escape it.'

She shuddered, 'I have been within an inch of my life, and didn't know it!'

'You have been perfectly safe, nevertheless. My sword never errs.' And Troy returned the weapon to the scabbard.

Bathsheba, overcome by a hundred tumultuous feelings resulting from the scene, abstractedly sat down on a tuft of heather.

'I must leave you now,' said Troy softly. 'And I'll venture to take and keep this in remembrance of you.'

She saw him stoop to the grass, pick up the winding lock which he had severed from her manifold tresses, twist it round his fingers, unfasten a button in the breast of his coat, and carefully put it inside.

He drew near and said, 'I must be leaving you.' He drew nearer still. A minute later and she saw his scarlet form disappear amid the ferny thicket, almost in a flash, like a brand swiftly waved.

That minute's interval had brought the blood beating into her face. It had brought upon her a stroke resulting in a stream of tears. She felt like one who has sinned a great sin.

The circumstance had been the gentle dip of Troy's mouth downwards upon her own. He had kissed her.

CHAPTER TWENTY-FOUR

PARTICULARS OF A TWILIGHT WALK

Bathsheba loved Troy in the way that only self-reliant women love when they abandon their self-reliance. When a strong woman recklessly throws away her strength she is worse than a weak woman who has never had any strength to throw away. Weakness is doubly weak by being new.

Troy's deformities lay deep down from a woman's vision, whilst his embellishments were upon the very surface; thus contrasting with homely Oak, whose defects were patent to the blindest and whose virtues were as metals in a mine.

The difference between love and respect was markedly shown in her conduct. Bathsheba has spoken of her interest in Boldwood with the greatest freedom to Liddy, but she had only communed with her own heart concerning Troy.

All this infatuation Gabriel saw, and was troubled thereby.

That is a noble though perhaps an unpromising love which not even the fear of breeding aversion in the bosom of the one beloved can deter from combating his or her errors. Oak determined to speak to his mistress. He would base his appeal on what he considered her unfair treatment of Farmer Boldwood, now absent from home.

An opportunity occurred one evening when she had gone for a short walk by a path through the neighbouring cornfields. It was dusk when Oak, who had not been far afield that day, took the same path and met her returning, quite pensively, as he thought.

'Oh, is it Gabriel?' she said. 'You are taking a walk too. Goodnight.'

'I thought I would come to meet you as it is rather late,' said Oak, turning and following at her heels. 'And as the man who would naturally come to meet you is away from home, too—I mean Farmer Boldwood—why, thinks I, I'll go,' he said.

'I don't quite understand what you mean by saying that Mr Boldwood would naturally come to meet me.'

'I mean on account of the wedding which they say is likely to take place between you and him, miss. Forgive my speaking plainly.'

'They say what is not true,' she returned quickly. 'No marriage is likely to take place between us.'

Gabriel now put forth his unobscured opinion, for the moment had come. 'Well, Miss Everdene,' he said, 'putting aside what people say, I never in my life saw any courting if his is not a courting of you.'

'Since this subject has been mentioned,' she said very emphatically, 'I am glad of the opportunity of clearing up a mistake which is very common and very provoking. I didn't definitely promise Mr Boldwood anything. I have never cared for him. I respect him, and he has urged me to marry him. But I have given him no distinct answer, and when I do so the answer will be that I cannot think of marrying him.'

Oak was unfortunately led on to speak of Boldwood's rival in a wrong tone to her after all. 'I wish you had never met that young Sergeant Troy, miss,' he sighed.

Bathsheba's steps became faintly spasmodic. 'Why?' she asked.

'He is not good enough for 'ee.'

'Why, pray?'

'I like soldiers, but this one I do not like,' he said sturdily.

'His cleverness in his calling may have tempted him astray, and what is mirth to the neighbours is ruin to the woman.'

'I say—I say again—that it doesn't become you to talk about him. Why he should be mentioned passes me quite!' she exclaimed desperately. 'He's good as anybody in this parish! He is very particular too, about going to church—yes, he is!'

'I am afraid nobody ever saw him there. I never did, certainly.'

'The reason of that is,' she said eagerly, 'that he goes in privately by the old tower door, just when the service commences, and sits at the back of the gallery. He told me so.'

Oak was grieved to find how entirely she trusted him. He brimmed with deep feeling as he replied in a steady voice, the steadiness of which was spoilt by the palpableness of his great effort to keep it so:—

'You know, mistress, that I love you, and shall love you always. I only mention this to bring to your mind that at any rate I would wish to do you no harm: beyond that I put it aside. I have lost in the race for money and good things, and I am not such a fool as to pretend to 'ee now I am poor, and you have got altogether above me. But Bathsheba, dear mistress, this I beg you to consider—that both to keep yourself well honoured among the workfolk, and in common generosity to an honourable man who loves you as well as I, you should be more discreet in your bearing towards this soldier.'

Oak's allusion to his own love for her lessened, to some extent, her anger at his interference; but she could not really forgive him for letting his wish to marry her be eclipsed by his wish to do her good, any more than for his slighting treatment of Troy.

She said, 'Will you leave me alone? I don't order it as a mistress—I ask it as a woman, and I expect you not to be so uncourteous as to refuse.'

'Certainly I will, Miss Everdene,' said Gabriel gently. He stood still and allowed her to get far ahead of him till he could only see her form upon the sky.

He saw a figure rise, apparently from the earth beside her. The shape beyond all doubt was Troy's. Oak would not be even a possible listener, and at once turned back till a good two hundred yards were between the lovers and himself.

Gabriel went home by way of the churchyard. In passing the tower he thought of what she had said about the sergeant's virtuous habit of entering the church unperceived at the beginning of service. Believing that the little gallery door alluded to was quite disused, he ascended the external flight of steps at the top of which it stood. A sprig of ivy had grown from the wall across the door to a length of more than a foot, delicately tying the panel to the stone jamb. It was a decisive proof that the door had not been opened at least since Troy came back to Weatherbury.

CHAPTER TWENTY-FIVE

HOT CHEEKS AND TEARFUL EYES

Half an hour later Bathsheba entered her own house. There burnt upon her face when she met the light of the candles the flush and excitement which were little less than chronic with her now. The farewell words of Troy still lingered in her ears. He had bidden her adieu for two days, which were so he stated, to be spent at Bath in visiting some friends. He had also kissed her a second time.

She now sank into a chair, wild and perturbed by all these new and fevering sequences. Then she jumped up with a manner of decision.

In three minutes, without pause or modification, she had written a letter to Boldwood, at his address beyond Casterbridge, saying mildly but firmly she had well considered the whole subject he had brought before her and kindly given her time to decide upon; that her final decision was that she could not marry him. She arose to take the letter to any one of the women who might be in the kitchen.

She paused in the passage. A dialogue was going on in the kitchen, and Bathsheba and Troy were the subject of it.

Bathsheba burst in upon them.

'Who are you speaking of?' she asked.

There was a pause. At last Liddy said frankly, 'What was passing was a bit of a word about yourself, miss.'

'I thought so! You know I don't care in the least for Mr Troy—not I. Everybody knows how much I hate him. Yes, hate him!'

'I hate him too,' said Maryann.

'Maryann—Oh you perjured woman! How can you speak that wicked story!' said Bathsheba excitedly. 'You admired him from your heart only this morning!'

'Yes Miss, but so did you. He is a wild scamp now, and you are right to hate him.'

'He's *not* a wild scamp! I have no right to hate him, nor you, nor anybody. Mind this, if any of you say a word against him you'll be dismissed instantly!'

She surged back into the parlour, with a big heart and tearful eyes, Liddy following her.

'O miss!' said mild Liddy looking pitifully into Bathsheba's face. 'I am sorry we mistook you so! I did think you cared for him but I see you don't, now. People always say such foolery.'

Bathsheba burst out: 'O Liddy, are you such a simpleton? Can't you read riddles? Can't you see? Are you a woman yourself?'

Liddy's clear eyes rounded with wonderment.

'Yes; you must be a blind thing, Liddy!' she said in reckless abandonment and grief. 'O I love him to very distraction and misery and agony! Liddy, solemnly swear to me that he's not a fast man; that it is all lies they say about him!'

'But miss, how can I say he is not if—'

'You graceless girl! How can you have the cruel heart to repeat what they say? He *cannot be* bad, as is said—do you hear?'

'I don't know what to say, miss,' said Liddy, beginning to cry.

'Say you don't believe it—say you don't!'

'I don't believe him to be so bad as they make out.'

'He is not bad at all . . . My poor life and heart, how weak I am!' she moaned, heedless of Liddy's presence. 'O, how I wish I had never seen him! Loving is misery for women always. Dearly I am beginning to pay for the honour of owning a pretty face!'

CHAPTER TWENTY-SIX

BLAME – FURY

The next evening, Bathsheba, with the idea of getting out of the way of Mr Boldwood in the event of his returning to answer her note in person, proceeded to fulfil an engagement made with Liddy some few hours earlier.

She had walked nearly two miles of her journey, watching how the day was retreating, when she beheld advancing over Yalbury hill the very man she sought so anxiously to elude. Boldwood was stepping on, not with that quiet tread of reserved strength which was his customary gait, in which he always seemed to be balancing two thoughts. His manner was stunned and sluggish now.

He did not see Bathsheba till they were less than a stone's throw apart. He looked up at the sound of her pit-pat, and his changed appearance sufficiently denoted to her the depth and strength of the feelings paralysed by her letter.

'Oh; is it you, Mr Boldwood?' she faltered, a guilty warmth pulsing in her face.

Seeing she turned a little aside, he said, 'What, are you afraid of me?'

'Why should you say that?' said Bathsheba.

'I fancied you looked so,' said he. 'And it is most strange, because of its contrast with my feeling for you.'

She regained self-possession, fixed her eyes calmly, and waited.

'You know what that feeling is,' continued Boldwood deliberately. 'A thing strong as death. No dismissal by a hasty letter affects that.'

Bathsheba was unable to direct her will into any definite groove for freeing herself from this fearfully awkward position. She confusedly said, 'Good evening,' and was moving on. Boldwood walked up to her heavily and dully.

'Bathsheba—darling—is it final indeed?'

'Indeed it is.'

'O Bathsheba—have pity upon me!' Boldwood burst out.

'I am beyond myself about this, and am mad. I am no stoic at all to be supplicating here; but I do supplicate to you. I wish you knew what is in me of devotion to you; but it is impossible, that. In bare human mercy to a lonely man, don't throw me off now! You are the first woman of any shade or nature that I have ever looked at to love, and it is the having been so near claiming you for my own that makes this denial so hard to bear. How nearly you promised me!'

She checked emotion, looked him quietly and clearly in the face, and said in her low, firm voice, 'Mr Boldwood, I promised you nothing. Would you have had me a woman of clay when you paid me that furthest, highest compliment a man can pay a woman—telling her he loves her? I was bound to show some feeling, if I would not be a graceless shrew. Have reason, do, and think more kindly of me!'

'Well, never mind arguing—never mind. One thing is sure; you were all but mine, and now you are not nearly mine. Everything is changed, and that by you alone, remember. You were nothing to me once, and I was contented; you are now nothing to me again, and how different the second nothing is from the first! Dearest, dearest, say that you only wrote that refusal to me in fun—come say it to me.'

'It would be untrue. You overrate my capacity for love. I don't possess half the warmth of nature you believe me to have.'

'No, Miss Everdene. You are not the cold woman you would have me believe. No, no! It isn't because you have no feeling in you that you don't love me. You naturally would have me think so—you would hide from me that you have a burning heart like mine. You have love enough, but it is turned into a new channel. I know where.'

The swift music of her heart became hubbub now, and she throbbed to extremity. He was coming to Troy. He did then know what had occurred!

'Why did Troy not leave my treasure alone?' he asked fiercely.

'Before he worried you your inclination was to have me; when next I should have come to you your answer would have been Yes. Can you deny it—I ask, can you deny it?'

She delayed the reply, but was too honest to withhold it. 'I cannot,' she whispered.

'Then curse him; and curse him!' said Boldwood breaking into a whispered fury. 'Ah, a time of his life shall come when he will have to repent and think wretchedly of the pain he has caused another man; and then may he ache, and wish, and curse, and yearn—as I do now!'

'Don't, don't, O, don't pray down evil upon him!' she implored in a miserable cry. 'O, be kind to him, sir, for I love him true!'

Boldwood's ideas had reached that point of fusion at which outline and consistency entirely disappear. He did not hear her at all now.

'I'll punish him—by my soul, that will I! I'll meet him, soldier or no, and I'll horsewhip the untimely stripling for this reckless theft of my one delight. I pray God he may not come into my sight, for I may be tempted beyond myself. O, Bathsheba, keep him away—yes, keep him away from me!'

For a moment Boldwood stood inert. He then turned his face away, and withdrew, and his form was soon covered over by the twilight.

Bathsheba, who had been standing motionless as a model all this latter time, flung her hands to her face, and wildly attempted to ponder on the exhibition which had just passed away. In her distraction, she walked up and down, pressing her brow, and sobbing brokenly to herself. Then she sat down on a heap of stones by the wayside to think. There she remained long.

Bathsheba's perturbed meditations ultimately evolved a conclusion that there were only two remedies for the present desperate state of affairs. The first was merely to keep Troy from Weatherbury till Boldwood's indignation had cooled; the second to listen to Oak's entreaties, and Boldwood's denunciations, and give up Troy altogether.

It was a picture full of misery, but for a while she contemplated it firmly inflicting upon herself gratuitous tortures by imagining Troy the lover of another woman after forgetting her; for she had penetrated his nature so far as to estimate his tendencies pretty accurately, but unfortunately loved him no less in thinking that he might soon cease to love her—indeed, considerably more.

She jumped to her feet. She would see him at once. Yes, she would implore him by word of mouth to assist her in this dilemma. A letter to keep him away could not reach him in time, even if he should be disposed to listen to it.

It was now dark, and the hour must have been nearly ten. Her plan was to drive to Bath during the night, see Sergeant Troy in the morning before he set out to come to her, bid him farewell, and dismiss him: then to rest the horse thoroughly (herself to weep the while, she thought), starting early the next morning on her return journey.

CHAPTER TWENTY-SEVEN

IN THE SUN—A HARBINGER

A note came for Maryann, stating that business had called for mistress to Bath, but that she hoped to return in the course of the week.

Two weeks passed. The oat-harvest began, and all the men were a-field. Nothing was to be heard save the whetting of scythes and the hiss of tress oat-ears rubbing together.

The men saw a figure in a blue coat and brass buttons running to them across the field.

''Tis Cain' Ball,' said Gabriel.

'He's dressed up in his best clothes,' said Matthew Moon. He hev been away from home for a few days, since he's had that felon upon his finger: for 'a said, since I can't work I'll have a hollerday.'

By this time Cainy was nearing the group of harvesters, and was perceived to be carrying a large slice of bread and ham in one hand, from which he took mouthfuls as he ran, the other being wrapped in a bandage. When he came close, he began to cough violently.

'I've been visiting to Bath because I had a felon on my thumb; yes, and I've seen—ahok-ahok!'

Directly Cain mentioned Bath , they all threw down their hooks and forks and drew round him . 'Yes,' he continued, 'I've seed the world at last—yes—and I've seed our mis'ess—ahok-hok-hok!'

'Well, at Bath you saw—' prompted Gabriel.

'I saw our mistress,' continued the junior shepherd, 'and a sojer, walking along. And bymeby they got closer and closer and then went arm-in-crook, like courting complete—hok hok!'

'Now then,' said Gabriel impatiently, 'what did you see, Cain?'

'I seed our mis'ess go into a sort of a park place where there's seats, and shrubs and flowers, arm-in-crook with a sojer;' continued Cainy firmly, and with a dim sense that his words were very effective as regarded Gabriel's emotions. 'And I think the sojer was Sergeant Troy. And they sat there together for more than half-an-hour, talking moving things, and she once was crying 'most to death. And when they came out her eyes were shining and she was as white as a lily; and they looked into one another's faces, as far gone friendly as a man and woman can be.'

'Miss Everdene and the soldier were walking about together, you say?'

'Ay, and she wore a beautiful gold-colour silk gown, and when the sun shone upon the bright gown and his red coat—my! how handsome they looked. You could see'em all the length of the street.'

'And what then?' murmured Gabriel.

'And then—I didn't see no more of Miss Everdene at all.'

'Now, Cain Ball,' said Gabriel restlessly, 'can you swear in the most awful form that the woman you saw was Miss Everdene?

'Please no, Mister Oak!' said Cainy, looking from one to the other with great uneasiness at the spiritual magnitude of the position. 'I don't mind saying 'tis true, but I don't like to say 'tis damn true, if that's what you mane. All I mane is that in common truth 'twas Miss Everdene and Sergeant Troy, but in the horrible so-help-me truth that ye want to make of it perhaps 'twas somebody else!'

'There's no getting at the rights of it,' said Gabriel turning to his work.

Then the reapers' hooks were flourished again, and the old sounds went on. Gabriel, without making any pretence of being lively, did nothing to show that he was particularly dull. However, Coggan, who knew pretty nearly how the land lay, said—

'Don't take on about her, Gabriel. What difference does it make whose sweetheart she is, since she can't be yours?'

'That's the very thing I say to myself,' said Gabriel.

CHAPTER TWENTY-EIGHT

HOME AGAIN—A TRICKSTER

That same evening Gabriel was leaning over Coggan's garden-gate, before retiring to rest.

A vehicle of some kind was softly creeping along the lane. It was Miss Everdene's gig, and Liddy and her mistress were the only occupants.

The exquisite relief of finding that she was here again, safe and sound, overpowered all reflection, and Oak could only luxuriate in the sense of it. All grave reports, were forgotten.

Gabriel might have been there an additional half-hour when a dark form walked slowly by. 'Goodnight, Gabriel,' the passer said.

It was Boldwood. 'Goodnight, sir,' said Gabriel.

Farmer Boldwood went on to Miss Everdene's house. He had come to apologize and beg forgiveness of her with something like a sense of shame at his violence, having but just now learnt that she had returned—only from a visit to Liddy, as he supposed, the Bath episode being quite unknown to him.

He enquired for Miss Everdene.

Liddy came out and said, 'My mistress cannot see you, sir.' The farmer instantly went out by the gate. He was unforgiven—that was the issue of it all. He did not hurry homeward. A little distance from the house he caught sight of a scarlet and gilded form. Boldwood stepped forward.

'Sergeant Troy?'

'Yes—I'm Sergeant Troy.'

'I am William Boldbood. I wish to speak a word with you—about her who lives just ahead there—and about a woman you have wronged.'

'I wonder at your impertinence,' said Troy, moving on.

'Now look here,' said Boldwood, 'wonder or not, you are going to hold a conversation with me.'

Troy heard the dull determination in Boldwood's voice, looked at his stalwart frame, then at the thick cudgel he carried in his hand. It seemed worth while to be civil to Boldwood.

'Very well, I'll listen with pleasure,' said Troy.

'Well then—I know a good deal concerning your—Fanny Robin's attachment to you. You ought to marry her.'

'I suppose I ought to. Indeed, I wish to, but I cannot.'

'Why?'

Troy was about to utter something hastily; he checked himself and said, 'I am too poor.'

Boldwood continued, 'I may as well speak plainly; and understand, I don't wish to express any opinion on your conduct. I intend a business transaction with you. I was engaged to be married to Miss Everdene. If you had not come I should certainly have been accepted by this time. If you had not seen her you might have been married to Fanny. So all I ask is, don't molest her any more. Marry Fanny. I will make it worth your while. Leave Weatherby this night and you shall, take fifty pounds with you.'

'I like Fanny best,' said Troy, 'and I have all to gain by accepting your money and marrying Fan. Fifty pounds at once, you said?'

'Here they are,' Boldwood handed Troy a small packet.

A light pit pat was heard upon the road just above him.

'By George—'tis Bathsheba,' Troy said. 'She was expecting me tonight—and I must now speak to her and wish her goodbye according to your wish.'

'I don't see the necessity of speaking.'

'If she does not know what has become of me, she will think more about me than if I tell her flatly I have come to give her up.'

'Will you confine your words to that one point? Shall I hear every word you say?'

'Every word. Now be still, and mark what you hear.'

The light footstep came closer. Troy whistled a double note in a soft fluty tone.

'Frank dearest, is that you?' The tones were Bathsheba's.

'O God!' said Boldwood.

'Yes,' said Troy to her.

'How late you are,' she continued tenderly. 'Frank, it is so lucky! There's not a soul in my house but me tonight. Liddy wanted to go to her grandfather's and I said she might stay with them till tomorrow—when you'll be gone again.'

'Capital,' said Troy. 'But I had better go back for my bags; you run home while I fetch it, and I'll promise to be in your parlour in ten minutes.'

'Yes.' She turned and tripped back to the house.

During the progress of this dialogue there was a nervous twitching of Boldwood's tightly closed lips, and his face became bathed in a clammy dew. He now started forward towards Troy.

'Shall I tell her that I have come to give her up and cannot marry her?' said the soldier mockingly.

'No no; wait a minute. I want to say more to you,' said Boldwood, in a hoarse whisper. 'Troy, make her your wife, and don't act upon what I arranged just now. The alternative is dreadful, but take Bathsheba; I give her up! She must love you indeed to sell soul and body to you so utterly as she has done. Wretched woman—deluded woman—you are, Bathsheba!'

'But what about Fanny?'

'Troy,' said Boldwood imploringly, 'I'll do anything for you, only don't desert Bathsheba; pray don't desert her, Troy. I have twenty-one more pounds with me. Here is the sum. But before I leave you I must have a paper signed—'

'First we'll call upon her. She must be consulted.'

'Very well, go on.'

They went to Bathsheba's house, Troy said. Wait here a moment.' Opening the door, he glided inside.

Boldwood waited. In two minutes a light appeared in the passage. Boldwood then saw that the chain had been fixed across the door. Troy appeared inside carrying a candlestick. He handed a folded newspaper through the slit between door and door-post, and put the candle close. 'That's the paragraph,' he said, placing his finger on a line.

Boldwood looked and read—

MARRIAGES

'On the 17th inst., at St Ambrose's Church, Bath, by the Rev. G. Mincing B.A., Francis Troy, only son of the late Edward Troy, Esq. M.D., of Weatherbury, and sergeant 11th Dragoon Guards, to Bathsheba, only surviving daughter of the late Mr John Everdene of Casterbridge.'

The paper fell from Boldwood's hands. Troy said—

'Now, Boldwood, yours is the ridiculous fate which always attends interference etween a man and his wife. Fanny has long ago left me. I don't know where she is. I have searched everywhere. You say you love Bathsheba; yet on the merest apparent evidence you instantly believe in her dishonour. A fig for such love! Now that I've taught you a lesson, take your money back again.' He threw the money into the road, closed the door and locked himself in.

Throughout the whole of that night Boldwood's dark form might have been seen walking about the hills and downs of Weatherbury.

CHAPTER TWENTY-NINE

AT AN UPPER WINDOW

It was very early the next morning—a time of sun and dew.

Just before the clock struck five Gabriel Oak and Coggan passed the village cross and went on together to the fields. They were yet barely in view of their mistress's house, when Oak fancied he saw the opening of a casement in one of the upper windows.

A handsome man leaned idly from the lattice. He looked east and then west, in the manner of one who makes a first morning survey. The man was Sergeant Troy. His red jacket was loosely thrown on, but not buttoned, and he had altogether the relaxed bearing of a soldier taking his ease.

Coggan spoke first, looking quietly at the window.

'She has married him!' he said. He glanced round upon Gabriel. 'Good heavens above us, Oak, how white your face is; you look like a corpse! Lean on the gate: I'll wait a bit.'

'All right, all right.'

They stood by the gate awhile, Gabriel listlessly staring at the ground. His mind sped into the future, and saw there enacted in years of leisure the scenes of repentance that would ensure from this work of haste. That they were married he had instantly decided. Why had it been so mysteriously managed? It was not Bathsheba's way to do things furtively. With all her faults she was candour itself. Could she have been entrapped?

In a few minutes they moved on again towards the house. The sergeant still looked from the window.

'Morning comrades!' he shouted, in a cheery voice when they came up.

Coggan replied to the greeting. 'Bain't ye going to answer the man?' he then said to Gabriel.

Gabriel soon decided that, since the deed was done, to put the best face upon the matter would be the greatest kindness to her he loved.

'Good morning, Sergeant Troy,' he returned, in a ghastly voice.

'A rambling, gloomy house this,' said Troy, smiling.

'But it is a nice old house,' said Gabriel.

'Yes—I suppose so; but I feel like new wine in an old bottle here. I am for making this place more modern, that we may be cheerful while we can.'

Gabriel and Coggan began to move on.

'Here's half-a-crown to drink my health, men.' Troy threw the coin dexterously across the front plot and over the fence towards Gabriel, who shunned it in its fall, his face turning to an angry red. Coggan twirled his eye, edged forward, and caught the money.

'Very well—you keep it, Coggan,' said Gabriel with disdain and almost fiercely. 'As for me, I'll do without gifts from him!'

'Don't show it too much,' said Coggan musingly. 'For if he's married to her, he'll buy his discharge and be our master here. Therefore 'tis well to say "Friend" outwardly, though you say "Troublehouse" within.'

'Well—perhaps it is best to be silent; but I can't go further than that. I can't flatter, and if my place here is only to be kept by smoothing him down, my place must be lost.'

A horseman, whom they had for some time seen in the distance, now appeared close beside them.

'There's Mr Boldwood,' said Oak.

Coggan and Oak nodded respectfully to the farmer, just checked their paces to discover if they were wanted, and finding they were not, stood back to let him pass on.

The only signs of the terrible sorrow Boldwood had been combating through the night, and was combating now, were the want of colour in his well-defined face, the enlarged appearance of the veins in his forehead and temples, and the sharper lines about his mouth. Gabriel for a minute, rose above his own grief in noticing Boldwood's. He saw the square figure sitting erect upon the horse, the head turned to neither side, the elbows steady by the hips, the brim of the hat level and undisturbed in its onward glide, until the keen edges of Boldwood's shape sank by degrees over the hill.

CHAPTER THIRTY

WEALTH IN JEOPARDY—THE REVEL

One night, at the end of August, when Bathsheba's experiences as a married woman were still new, and when the weather was yet dry and sultry, a man stood motionless in the stackyard of Weatherbury Upper Farm, looking at the moon and sky.

The night had a sinister aspect. Thunder was imminent, and taking some secondary appearances into consideration, it was likely to be followed by one of the lengthened rains which mark the close of the dry weather for the season. Before twelve hours had passed a harvest atmosphere would be a bygone thing.

Oak glanced with misgiving at eight naked and unprotected ricks, massive and heavy with the rick produce on one half of the farm for that year. He went on to the barn.

This was the night selected by Sergeant Troy—ruling now in the room of his wife—for giving the harvest supper and dance.

As Oak approached the building the sounds of violins and a tambourine grew more distinct. He came close to the large doors and looked in.

The central space was appropriated for the dancers, and immediately opposite to Oak a rostrum had been erected, bearing a table and chairs. Here sat three fiddlers.

Gabriel avoided Bathsheba, and got as near as possible to the platform, where Sergeant Troy was seated, drinking brandy-and-water. Gabriel could not easily thrust himself within speaking distance of the Sergeant, and he sent a message, asking him to come down a moment. The sergeant said he could not attend.

'Well you tell him, then,' said Gabriel, 'that I only stepped ath'art to say that a heavy rain is sure to fall soon, and that something should be done to protect the ricks?'

'Mr Troy says it will not rain,' returned the messenger, 'and he cannot stop to talk with you about such fidgets.'

In juxtaposition with Troy, Oak had a melancholy tendency to look like a candle beside gas, and ill at ease he went out again.

At the door he paused for a moment. Troy was speaking.

'Friends,' he said. 'we'll send the women-folk home. 'Tis time they were in bed. Then we cockbirds will have a jolly carouse to ourselves!'

Bathsheba indignantly left the barn, followed by all the women and children. Thus Troy and the men on the farm were left sole occupants of the place. Oak, not to appear unnecessarily disagreeable, stayed a little while; then he, too, arose and quietly took his departure.

Gabriel proceeded towards his home. In approaching the door his toe kicked something which felt and sounded soft, leathery, and distended, like a boxing glove. It was a large toad humbly travelling across the path. He knew what this direct message from the Great Mother meant. And soon came another.

When he struck a light indoors there appeared on the table a think glistening streak. Oak's eyes followed the serpentine sheen to the other side, where it led up to a huge brown garden-slug, which had come indoors tonight for reasons of its own. It was Nature's way of hinting to him that he was to prepare for foul weather.

Oak sat down meditating for nearly an hour. It occurred to him that if there was one class of manifestation on this matter that he thoroughly understood, it was the instincts of the sheep. He left the room and ran across two or three fields towards the flock.

They were crowded close together around some bushes, grouped in such a way that their tails, without a single exception, were towards that half of the horizon from which the storm threatened.

This was enough to reestablish him in his original opinion. He knew now that he was right, and that Troy was wrong.

Oak returned to the stackyard. The conical tips of the ricks jutted darkly into the sky. There were five wheat ricks in this yard, and three stacks of barley. Oak mentally calculated their value to Bathsheba. Seven hundred and fifty pounds in the divinest form that money can wear—that of necessary food for man and beast; should the risk be run of deteriorating this bulk of corn to less than half its value because of the instability of a woman? 'Never, if I can prevent it!' said Gabriel.

Such was the argument that Oak set outwardly before him. It is possible that there was this golden legend under the utilitarian one: 'I will help to my last effort the woman I have loved so dearly'.

He went back to the barn to obtain assistance for covering the ricks that very night. An unusual picture met his eye.

The candles had burnt down to their sockets, and many of the lights had quite gone out. Here, under the table and leaning against forms and chairs were the wretched person of all the workfolk. In the midst of these shone red and distinct the figure of Sergeant Troy, leaning back in a chair.

Gabriel glanced hopelessly at the group. He saw at once that if the ricks were to be saved that night, he must save them with his own hands. He closed the door upon the men in their deep oblivious sleep, and went again out into the lone night.

Going on to Laban Tall's house in the village, Oak went round to the back door which had been left unfastened for Laban's entry, and took the key of the granary. Ten minutes later his lonely figure might have been seen dragging four large waterproof coverings across the yard, and two of these heaps of treasure in grain were covered snug—two cloths to each. Three wheat sacks remained open, and there were no more cloths. Oak found a fork. He mounted the third pile of wealth and began operating, adopting the plan of sloping the upper sheaves one over the other; and, in addition filling the interstices with the material of some untied sheaves.

So far all was well. By this hurried contrivance Bathsheba's property in wheat was safe for any rate a week or two, provided always that there was not much wind.

Next came the barley. This it was only possible to protect by systematic thatching. Time went on, and the moon vanished not to reappear.

CHAPTER THIRTY-ONE

THE STORM – THE TWO TOGETHER

A light flapped over the scene and a rumble filled the air. It was the first move of the approaching storm.

The second peal was noisy, with comparatively little visible lightning. Then came a third flash. The lightning now was the colour of silver, and gleamed in the heavens like a mailed army. Rumbles became rattles.

Gabriel felt his position to be anything but a safe one, and he took a precaution. Under the staddles was a long tethering chain, used to prevent the escape of errant horses. This he carried up the ladder, and sticking his rod through the clog at one end, allowed the other end of the chain to train on the ground. The spike attached to it he drove in. Under the shadow of this ex-temporised lightning-conductor he felt himself comparatively safe.

Out leapt another flash. In the open ground before him as he looked over the ridge of the rick, was a dark and apparently female form.

'Is that you, ma'am?' said Gabriel to the darkness.

'Who is there?' said the voice of Bathsheba.

'Gabriel, I am on the rick, thatching.'

'O, Gabriel!'—and are you? I have come about them. The weather awoke me, and I thought of the corn. I am so distressed about it—can we save it anyhow? I cannot find my husband. Do you know where he is?'

'Asleep in the barn.'

'He promised that the stacks should be seen to, and now they are all neglected! Can I do anything to help?'

'You can bring up some reed sheaves to me, one by one, ma'am; if you are not afraid to come up the ladder in the dark,' said Gabriel.

'I'll do anything!' she said resolutely. She instantly took a sheaf upon her shoulder, clambered up close to his heels, placed it behind the rod, and descended for another. At her third ascent the rick suddenly brightened with a flash from the east behind them.

Then came the peal. It was hardly credible that such a heavenly light could be the parent of such a diabolical sound. 'How terrible!' she exclaimed, and clutched him by the sleeve. Gabriel turned, and steadied her on her aerial perch by holding her arm.

The next flare came. Heaven opened then, indeed. The flash was almost too novel for its inexpressibly dangerous nature to be at once realised, and they could only comprehend the magnificence of its beauty. It sprang from east, west, north, south, and it was a perfect dance of death. Simultaneously came from every part of the trembling sky what was more of the nature of a shout than anything else earthly. Gabriel was almost blinded, and he could feel Bathsheba's warm arm tremble in his hand—a sensation novel and thrilling enough; but love, life, everything human, seemed small and trifling in such close juxtaposition with an infuriated universe.

Oak had hardly time to gather up these impressions into a thought, when the tall tree on the hill seemed on fire to a white heat. The tree was sliced down the whole length of its tall, straight stem, a huge riband of bark being apparently flung off. The other portion remained erect, and revealed the bared surface of the white down the front. The lightning had struck the tree. A sulphurous smell filled the air; then all was silent, and black as a cave.

'We had a narrow escape!' said Gabriel hurriedly. 'You had better go down.'

She descended the ladder, and, on second thoughts, he followed her. The darkness was impenetrable by the sharpest vision. They both stood still at the bottom side by side. Bathsheba appeared to think only of the weather—Oak thought only of her just then. At last he said—

'The storm seems to have passed now, at any rate. I cannot understand no rain falling. But heaven be praised, it is all the better for us. I am going up again.'

'Gabriel, you are kinder than I deserve! I will stay and help you yet.'

He remarked gently, 'If you'll hand up a few more, miss—ma'am, it would save much time.'

Then Oak ascended to the top, and went on thatching. She followed, but without a sheaf.

'Gabriel,' she said in a strange and impressive voice.

Oak looked up at her, 'Yes, mistress,' he said.

'I suppose you thought that when I galloped away to Bath that night it was on purpose to be married?'

'I did at last—not at first,' he answered, somewhat surprised at the abruptness with which this new subject was broached.

'I thought so. Now, I care a little for your good opinion and I want to explain something—I have longed to do it ever since I returned, and you looked so gravely at me. For if I were to die—and I may die soon—it would be dreadful that you should always think mistakenly of me. Now, listen.'

Gabriel ceased his rustling.

'I went to Bath that night in the full intention of breaking off my engagement to Mr Troy. It was owing to circumstances which occurred after I got there that—that we were married. Now do you see the matter in a new light?'

'I do, somewhat.'

'I must, I suppose, say more, now that I have begun. Well, I was alone in a strange city, and the horse was lame. And at last I didn't know what to do. I saw, when it was too late, that scandal might seize hold of me for meeting him alone in that way. But I was coming away, when he suddenly said he had that day seen a woman more beautiful than I, and that his constancy could not be counted on unless I became his . . . And I was grieved and troubled—' She cleared her voice, and waited a moment, as if to gather breath. 'And then, between jealousy and distraction, I married him!' she whispered with desperate impetuosity.

Gabriel made no reply.

She went down the ladder and the work proceeded. Gabriel soon perceived a languor in the movements of his mistress up and down, and he said to her, gently as a mother—

'I think you had better go indoors now, you are tired. I can finish the rest alone.'

'Thank you for your devotion, a thousand times, Gabriel!' she said gratefully. 'Goodnight—I know you are doing your very best for me.'

Gabriel worked in a reverie which was disturbed by the grating noise of the vane on the roof turning round, and this change in the wind was a signal for rain.

CHAPTER THIRTY-TWO

COMING HOME – A CRY

On the turnpike road, between Casterbridge and Weatherbury, is one of those steep long ascents which pervade the highways of this undulating part of South Wessex.

One Saturday evening in the month of October Bathsheba's vehicle was duly creeping up this incline. She was sitting listlessly in the second seat of the gig, whilst walking beside her in a farmer's marketing suit of unusually fashionable cut was an erect, well-made young man. This man was her husband, formerly Sergeant Troy, who, having bought his discharge with Bathsheba's money, was gradually transforming himself into a farmer of a spirited and very modern school.

'Yes, if it hadn't been for that wretched rain I should have cleared two hundred as easy as looking, my love,' he was saying 'Don't you see, it altered all the chances? The fact is, these autumn races are the ruin of everybody.'

'And you mean, Frank,' said Bathsheba sadly, 'that you have lost more than a hundred pounds in a month by this dreadful horse-racing? O, Frank, it is cruel; it is foolish of you to take away my money so. We shall have to leave the farm; that will be the end of it!'

'There now, don't you be a little fool. Why, Bathsheba, you have lost all the pluck and sauciness you formerly had and upon my life if I had known what a chicken-hearted creature you were under all your boldness, I'd never have—I know what.'

A flash of indignation might have been in Bathsheba's dark eyes as she looked resolutely ahead after this reply. They moved on without further speech.

A woman appeared on the brow of the hill. Troy had turned towards the gig to remount, and the woman passed behind him.

Though the approach of eventide enveloped them in gloom, Bathsheba could see plainly enough to discern the extreme poverty of the woman's garb, and the sadness of her face.

'Please, sir, do you know at what time Casterbridge Union-house closes at night?'

The woman said these words to Troy over his shoulder.

Troy started visibly at the sound of the voice; yet he seemed to recover presence of mind sufficient to prevent himself from giving way to his impulse to suddenly turn and face her. He said, slowly—

'I don't know.'

The woman, on hearing him speak, quickly looked up, examined the side of his face, and recognised the soldier under the yeoman's garb. Her face was drawn into an expression which had gladness and agony both among its elements. She uttered a hysterical cry, and fell down.

'O, poor thing!' exclaimed Bathsheba, instantly preparing to alight.

'Stay where you are, and attend to the horse!' said Troy peremptorily, throwing her the reins and the whip. 'Walk the horse to the top: I'll see to the woman.'

'But I—'

'Do you hear? Clk—poppet!'

The horse, gig, and Bathsheba moved on.

'How on earth did you come here? I thought you were miles away, or dead! Why didn't you write to me?' said Troy to the woman, in a strangely gentle, yet hurried voice, as he lifted her up.

'I feared to.'

'Have you any money?'

'None.'

'Good Heaven—I wish I had more to give you!' Here's—wretched—the merest trifle. It is every farthing I have left.'

The woman made no answer.

'I have only another moment,' continued Troy; 'and now listen. Where are you going to-night? Casterbridge Union?'

'Yes; I thought to go there.'

'Sleep there tonight, and stay there tomorrow. Monday is the first free day I have; and on Monday morning, at ten exactly, meet me on Grey's Bridge, just out of the town. I'll bring all the money I can muster. You shan't want—I'll see that, Fanny: then I'll get you a lodging somewhere. Goodbye till then. I am a brute—but goodbye!'

Troy then came on towards his wife. He was rather agitated.

'Do you know who that woman was?' said Bathsheba, looking searchingly into his face.

'I do,' he said, looking boldly back into hers.

'Who is she?'

He suddenly seemed to think that frankness would benefit neither of the women.

'Nothing to either of us. I know her by sight.'

No more was said.

For a considerable time the woman walked on. Her steps became feebler. At length her onward walk dwindled to the merest totter, and she opened a gate within which was a haystack. Underneath this she sat down and presently slept.

When the woman awoke it was to find herself in the depths of a moonless and starless night. A distant halo which hung over the town of Casterbridge was visible. Towards this weak, soft glow the woman turned her eyes.

'If only I could get there!' she said. 'Meet him the day after tomorrow: God help me! Perhaps I shall be in my grave before then!'

CHAPTER THIRTY-THREE

SUSPICION – FANNY IS SENT FOR

Bathsheba said very little to her husband all that evening of their return from market, and he was not disposed to say much to her. The next day, which was Sunday, passed nearly in the same manner. This was the day before the Budmouth races. In the evening Troy said, suddenly—

'Bathsheba, could you let me have twenty pounds?'

'Ah! for those races to-morrow.'

'The money is not wanted for racing debts at all,' he said.

'What is it for?' she asked. 'You worry me a great deal by these mysterious responsibilities, Frank.'

'You wrong me by such a suspicious manner,' he said. 'Such strait-waistcoating as you treat me to is not becoming in you at so early a date.'

She gave a sigh of resignation. 'I have about that sum here for household expenses. If you must have it, take it.'

'Very good. Thank you. I expect I shall have gone away before you are in to breakfast tomorrow.' Troy, as he spoke, looked at his watch, and opened the case at the back, revealing, snugly stowed within it, a small coil of hair.

Bathsheba's eyes had been accidentally lifted at that moment, and she saw the action and saw the hair. She flushed in pain and surprise, and some words escaped her before she had thought whether or not it was wise to utter them. 'A woman's curl of hair!' she said. 'O, Frank whose is that?'

Troy had instantly closed his watch. He carelessly replied, as one who cloaked some feelings that the sight had stirred: 'Why, yours, of course. Whose should it be? I had quite forgotten that I had it.'

'That's insulting me. It was yellow hair. Now whose was it? I want to know.'

'Very well—I'll tell you, so make no more ado. It is the hair of a young woman I was going to marry before I knew you. Until to-day, when I took it from a drawer, I have never looked upon that bit of hair for several months—that I am ready to swear,' Troy said, rising as he did so, and leaving the room.

Directly he had gone, Bathsheba burst into great sobs—dry-eyed sobs, which cut as they came, without any softening by tears. But she determined to repress all evidences of feeling. Until she had met Troy, Bathsheba had been proud of her position as a woman; it had been a glory to her to know that her lips had been touched by no man's on earth—that her waist had never been encircled by a lover's arm. She hated herself now. O, if she had never stopped to folly of this kind, respectable as it was, and could only stand again, as she had stood on the hill at Norcombe, and dare Troy or any other man to pollute a hair of her head by his interference!

The next morning she rose earlier than usual, and had the horse saddled for her ride round the farm in the customary way. When she came in at half-past eight—their usual hour for breakfasting—she was informed that her husband had risen, taken his breakfast, and driven off to Casterbridge with the gig and Poppet.

After breakfast she was cool and collected—quite herself in fact—and she rambled to the gate, intending to walk to another quarter of the farm, which she still personally superintended.

She saw a man coming up the road, a man like Mr Boldwood. It was Mr Boldwood. Bathsheba blushed painfully, and watched. The farmer stopped when still a long way off, and held up his hand to Gabriel Oak, across the field. The two men then approached each other and seemed to engage in earnest conversation.

Joseph Poorgrass now passed near them. Boldwood and Gabriel called to him, spoke to him for a few minutes, and then all three parted, Joseph immediately coming up the hill with his barrow.

'Well, what's the message, Joseph? Bathsheba said

'You'll never see Fanny Robin no more, ma'am. She's dead in the Union.'

'Fanny dead—never!'

'Yes ma'am. She was took bad in the morning, and, being quite feeble and worn out, she died in the evening. Mr Boldwood is going to send a waggon to fetch her home here.'

'Indeed, I shall not let Mr Boldwood do any such thing. I shall do it! How very, very said this is!—the idea of Fanny being in a workhouse.' Bathsheba had begun to know what suffering was, and she spoke with real feeling . . . 'Joseph, have the new spring waggon with the blue body and red wheels, and wash it very clean. And, carry with you some evergreens and flowers to put upon the coffin.'

'I will, ma'am.'

'Casterbridge Union—' said Bathsheba, musing. 'I wish I had known of it sooner. I thought she was far away. How long has she lived there?'

'Only been there a day or two. She's been picking up a living at seampstering in Melchester for several months. She only got handy the Union-house on Sunday morning 'a b'lieve, and 'tis supposed here and there that she had traipsed every step of the way from Melchester.'

'Ah-h!'

No gem ever flashed from a rosy ray to a white one more rapidly than changed the young wife's countenance whilst this word came from her in a long-drawn breath. 'Did she walk along our turnpike-road?' she said, in a suddenly restless and eager voice.

'I believe she did . . . Ma'am, shall I call Liddy? You bain't well, ma'am, surely? You look like a lily—so pale and fainty!'

'No; don't call her; it is nothing. When did she pass Weatherbury?'

'Last Saturday night.'

'Thank you, Joseph. That will do. Go on now, or you'll be late.'

Bathsheba, still unhappy, went indoors again. In the course of the afternoon she said to Liddy, 'What was the colour of poor Fanny Robin's hair? Do you know? I cannot recollect—I only saw her for a day or two.'

'It was light, ma'am. I have seen her let it down when she was going to bed, and it looked beautiful then. Real golden hair.'

CHAPTER THIRTY-FOUR

JOSEPH AND HIS BURDEN—BUCK'S HEAD

As the clock pointed to five minutes to three, a blue spring waggon, picked out with red, and containing boughs and flowers, approached Casterbridge Union-house. Joseph Poorgrass rang the bell. The door opened, and a plain elm coffin was slowly thrust forth, and laid by two men along the middle of the vehicle.

One of the men took from his pocket a lump of chalk, and wrote upon the cover a few words in a large scrawling hand. He covered the whole with a black cloth and handed a certificate of registry to Poorgrass. Both men entered the door, closing it behind them. Their connection with her, short as it had been, was over forever.

Joseph then placed the flowers as enjoined, and the evergreens around the flowers, till it was difficult to divine what the waggon contained; he smacked his whip, and the rather pleasing funeral car crept down the hill, and along the road to Weatherbury.

The afternoon drew on apace. It was a relief to Joseph's heart when the friendly signboard of the Buck's Head Inn came in view, and, stopping his horse immediately beneath it, he proceeded to fulfil an intention made a long time before. He turned the horse's head to the green bank, and entered the hostel for a mug of ale.

In the kitchen of the inn, what should Joseph see to gladden his eyes but the countenances of Mr Jan Coggan and Mr Mark Clark, the owners of the two most appreciative throats in the neighbourhood, within the pale of respectability.

'Why, 'tis neighbour Poorgrass!' said Mark Clark. 'I'm sure your face don't praise your mistress's table, Joseph.'

'I've had a very pale companion for the last four miles,' said Joseph, 'I assure ye, I ha'n't seed the colour of victuals or drink since breakfast time this morning.'

'Then drink, Joseph and don't restrain yourself!' said Coggan.

Joseph drank for a moderately long time, then for a longer time, saying, as he lowered the jug, 'Well, I must be on again, I've got poor little Fanny Robin in my waggon outside.'

'But what's yer hurry, Joseph? Sit down comfortable and finish another with us.'

'Well, I hope Providence won't be in a way with me for my doings,' said Joseph sitting down again.

The longer Joseph Poorgrass remained, the less his spirit was troubled by the duties which developed upon him this afternoon.

The minutes glided by uncounted, until Coggan's repeater struck six from his pocket in the usual still small tones.

At that moment hasty steps were heard in the entry and the door opened to admit the figure of Gabriel Oak. He stared sternly at the faces of the sitters. Joseph Poorgrass blinked, and shrank several inches into the background.

Gabriel, seeing that neither of the three was in a fit state to take charge of the waggon for the remainder of the journey, made no comment, but went across to where the vehicle stood. He pulled the horse's head and drove along through the unwholesome night.

By the time that Gabriel reached the old manor-house, it was quite dark. A man came from the gate and said through the fog—

'Is that Poorgrass with the corpse?'

Gabriel recognised the voice as that of the parson.

'The corpse is here, sir,' said Gabriel.

'I have just been to inquire of Mrs Troy if she could tell me the reason of the delay. I am afraid it is too late now for the funeral to be performed with proper decency. We'll put it off till tomorrow morning. The body may be brought on to the church, or it may be left here at the farm and fetched by the bearers in the morning.'

Gabriel had his reasons for thinking the latter a most objectionable plan. Visions of several unhappy contingencies which might arise from this delay flitted before him. But his will was not law and he went indoors to inquire of his mistress what were her wishes on the subject. Bathsheba desired that the girl might be brought into the house. Oak argued upon the convenience of leaving her in the waggon, just as she lay now, till the morning, but to no purpose. 'It is unkind and unchristian,' she said, 'to leave the poor thing in a coach house all night.'

Gabriel lighted a lantern. Fetching three other men to assist him, they bore the coffin indoors, placing it on two benches in the middle of a little sitting-room next to the hall, as Bathsheba directed.

Every one except Gabriel Oak then left the room. He still indecisively lingered beside the body. Suddenly, as in a last attempt to save Bathsheba from, at any rate, immediate anguish, he looked again, as he had looked before at the chalk writing upon the coffin-lid—'*Fanny Robin and Child*' Gabriel took his handkerchief and carefully robbed out of the two latter words, leaving visible one inscription '*Fanny Robin*' only. He left the room, and went out quietly by the front door.

CHAPTER THIRTY-FIVE

FANNY'S REVENGE

'Do you want me any longer, ma'am?' inquired Liddy, at a later hour the same evening, standing by the door and addressing Bathsheba, who sat cheerless and alone in the large parlour.

'No more tonight, Liddy . . . '

Bathsheba suddenly exclaimed in an impulsive and excited whisper, 'Have you heard anything strange said of Fanny?'

Bathsheba was lonely and miserable now; not lonelier actually than she had been before her marriage; but her loneliness then was to that of the present time as the solitude of a mountain is to the solitude of a cave. And within the last day or two had come these disquieting thoughts about her husband's past.

Liddy stood hesitating, until at length she said, 'Maryann has just heard something very strange. A wicked story is got to Weatherbury within this last hour—that—' Liddy came close to her mistress and whispered the remainder of the sentence slowly into her ear.

Bathsheba trembled from head to foot.

'I don't believe it!' she said excitedly. 'And there's only one name written on the coffin-cover.'

Bathsheba turned and looked into the fire, that Liddy might not see her face. Finding that the mistress was going to say no more, Liddy glided out, closed the door softly, and went to bed.

Bathsheba's face, as she continued looking into the fire that evening, might have excited solicitousness on her account even among those who loved her least.

She went to the door and opened it. She paused in the hall, looking at the door of the room wherein Fanny lay. She locked her fingers, threw back her head, and strained her hot hands rigidly across her forehead, saying, with a hysterical sob, 'Would to God you would speak and tell me your secret, Fanny! . . . O, I hope, hope it is not true that there are two of you! . . . if I could only look in upon you for one little minute, I should know all!'

A few moments passed, and she added, slowly, 'And I will.'

Bathsheba in after times could never gauge the mood which carried her through the actions following this murmured resolution on this memorable evening of her life. She went to the lumber-closet for a screw-driver. At the end of a short though undefined time she found herself in the small room, quivering with emotion, standing beside the uncovered coffin of the girl whose conjectured end had so entirely engrossed her, and saying to herself in a husky voice as she gazed within—

'It was best to know the worst, and I know it now!'

She knelt beside the coffin and covered her face with her hands.

She knew not how long she remained thus. She forgot time, life where she was, what she was doing. A slamming together of the coach-house doors in the yard brought her to herself again. An instant after, the front door opened and closed, steps crossed the hall, and her husband appeared at the entrance to the room looking in upon her.

At this moment, as he stood with the door in his hand, Troy never once thought of Fanny in connection with what he saw. His first confused idea was that somebody in the house had died.

'What's the matter, in God's name? Who's dead?' said Troy. He came up the room, and approached the coffin's side.

The candle was standing on a bureau close by them, and the light slanted down, distinctly enkindling the cold features of both mother and babe. Troy looked in, knowledge of it all come over him in a lurid sheen, and he stood still.

'Do you know her?' said Bathsheba, in a small enclosed echo, as from the interior of a cell.

'I do,' said Troy. 'I have been a bad, black-hearted man.'

He sank upon his knees with an indefinable union of remorse and reverence upon his face, and, bending over Fanny Robin, gently kissed her, as one would kiss an infant asleep to avoid awakening it. 'I should have married her. Would to God that I had; but it is all too late! I deserve to live in torment for this!' He turned to Fanny. 'But never mind, darling,' he said; 'in the sight of Heaven you are my very, very wife!'

At these words arose from Bathsheba's lips a long, low cry of measureless despair and indignation, such a wail of anguish as had never before been heard within those old-inhabited walls.

'If she's—that,—what—am I?' she added, as a continuation of the same cry, and sobbing pitifully; and the rarity with her of such abandonment only made the condition more dire.

'You are nothing to me—nothing,' said Troy heartlessly. 'A ceremony before a priest doesn't make a marriage. I am not morally yours.'

A vehement impulse to flee from him, to run from this place and hide mastered Bathsheba now. She waited not an instant, but turned to the door and ran out.

CHAPTER THIRTY-SIX

TROY'S ROMANTICISM

When Troy's wife left him his first act was to cover the dead from sight. This done he ascended the stairs, and throwing himself down upon the bed dressed as he was, he waited miserably for the morning.

Fate had dealt grimly with him through the last four-and-twenty hours. His day had been spent in a way which varied very materially from his intentions regarding it.

Twenty pounds having been secured from Bathsheba, he had managed to add to the sum every farthing he could muster on his own account, which had been seven pounds ten. With this money, he had hastily driven from the gate that morning to keep his appointment with Fanny Robin.

The clocks struck the hour, and no Fanny appeared. In fact, at that moment she was being robed in her grave-clothes by two attendants at the Union poor-house. The quarter went, the half hour. A rush of recollection came upon Troy as he waited: this was the second time she had broken a serious engagement with him. In anger he vowed it should be the last, and at eleven o'clock he drove on to Budmouth races.

He reached the race-course at two o'clock. But Fanny's image, as it had appeared to him in the sombre shadows of that Saturday evening, returned to his mind, backed up by Bathsheba's reproaches. He vowed he would not bet, and he kept his vow, for on leaving the town at nine o'clock in the evening he had diminished his cash only to the extent of a few shillings.

He trotted slowly homeward, and it was now that he was struck for the first time with a thought that Fanny had been really prevented by illness from keeping her promise. He regretted that he had not remained in Casterbridge and made inquiries. Reaching home he quietly unharnessed the horse and came indoors, as we have seen, to the fearful shock that awaited him.

As soon as it grew light enough to distinguish objects, Troy arose, stalked downstairs and left the house by the back door. His walk was towards the churchyard, entering which he searched around till he found a newly dug unoccupied grave—the grave dug for Fanny. The position of this having been marked, he hastened on to Casterbridge.

Reaching the town, Troy descended into a side street and entered a pair of gates surmounted by a board bearing the words, 'Lester, stone and marble mason.'

'I want a good tomb,' he said to the man who stood in the little office. 'I want as good a one as you can give me for twenty-seven pounds.'

It was all the money he possessed.

'That sum to include everything?'

'Everything. Cutting the name, carriage to Weatherbury, and erection. And I want it now, at once.'

'The best I have in stock is this one,' said the stone-cutter.

'Here's a marble headstone beautifully crocketed. The polishing alone of the set cost eleven pounds. I could add the name, and put it up at Weatherbury for the sum you mention.'

'Get it done today, and I'll pay the money now.'

The man agreed, and wondered at such a mood in a visitor who wore not a shred of mourning. Troy then wrote the words which were to form the inscription, settled the account and went away. In the afternoon he came back again, and found that the lettering was almost done. He waited in the yard till the tomb was packed, and saw it placed in the cart and starting on its way to Weatherbury, giving directions to the two men who were to accompany it to inquire of the sexton for the grave of the person named in the inscription.

The next morning Bathsheba resolved to go out and walk a little way. So when breakfast was over she put on her bonnet, and took a direction towards the church. Knowing that Fanny had been laid in the parish 'behind church,' it was impossible to resist the impulse to enter and look upon a spot which, from nameless feelings she at the same time dreaded to see.

Bathsheba did not at once perceive that the grand tomb was Fanny's and she looked for some humbler mound. Then she beheld the tomb and read the words with which the inscription opened:—'Erected by Francis Troy in Beloved Memory of Fanny Robin.'

CHAPTER THIRTY-SEVEN

ADVENTURES BY THE SHORE

Troy wandered along towards the south. A composite feeling, made up of disgust, remorse, and a general averseness to his wife's society, impelled him to seek a home in any place on earth save Weatherbury. The sad accessories of Fanny's end confronted him as vivid pictures which threatened to be indelible, and made life in Bathsheba's house intolerable.

He found himself near a small basin of sea enclosed by the cliffs. Troy's nature freshened within him; he thought he would rest and bathe here before going further. He undressed and plunged in. Inside the cove the water was uninteresting to a swimmer, being smooth as a pond, and to get a little of the ocean swell Troy presently swam between the two projecting spurs of rock. Unfortunately for Troy a current unknown to him existed outside, which was awkward for a swimmer who might be taken in it unawares. Troy found himself carried to the left and then round in a swoop out to sea.

Troy resolved as a last resource to tread water at a slight incline, and so endeavour to reach the shore at any point, merely giving himself a gentle impetus inwards whilst carried on in the general direction of the tide. This, necessarily a slow process, he found to be not altogether so difficult. Presently a ship's boat appeared, manned with several sailor lads, her bows towards the sea.

Swimming with his right arm, Troy held up his left to hail them, splashing upon the waves, and shouting with all his might.

The men saw him, and backing their oars and putting the boat about, they pulled towards him with a will. In five or six minutes from the time of his first halloo, two of the sailors hauled him in over the stern.

They formed part of a brig's crew, and had come ashore for sand. Lending him what little clothing they could spare among them as a slight protection against the rapidly cooling air, they agreed to land him in the morning; and without further delay, for it was growing late, they made again towards the roadstead where their vessel lay.

CHAPTER THIRTY-EIGHT

DOUBTS ARISE—DOUBTS LINGER

Bathsheba underwent the enlargement of her husband's absence from hours to days with a slight feeling of surprise, and a slight feeling of relief; yet neither sensation rose at any time far above the level commonly designated as indifference.

The first Saturday after Troy's departure she went to Casterbridge alone, a journey she had not before taken since her marriage. On this Saturday Bathsheba was passing slowly on foot through the crowd of rural businessmen gathered as usual in front of the market-house, when a man, who had apparently been following her, said some words to another on her left hand. Bathsheba distinctly heard what the speaker said, though her back was towards him.

'I am looking for Mrs Troy. Is that she there?'

'Yes; that's the young lady, I believe,' said the person addressed.

'I have some awkward news to break to her. Her husband is drowned.'

As if endowed with the spirit of prophecy, Bathsheba gasped out, 'No, it is not true; it cannot be true!' Then she said and heard no more. A darkness came into her eyes, and she fell.

But not to the ground. A gloomy man, who had been observing her from under the portico of the old corn-exchange when she passed through the group without, stepped quickly to her side at the moment of her exclamation, and caught her in his arms as she sank down.

'What is it?' said Boldwood, looking up at the bringer of the big news, as he supported her.

'Her husband was drowned this week while bathing in Lulwind Cove. A coastguardsmen found his clothes, and brought them into Budmouth yesterday.'

Thereupon a strange fire lighted up Boldwood's eye, and his face flushed with the suppressed excitement of an unutterable thought. Everybody's glance was now centred upon him and the unconscious Bathsheba. Soon she opened her eyes. Remembering all that had occurred, she murmured, 'I want to go home!'

Being hardly in a condition to drive home as she had driven to town, Boldwood, with every delicacy of manner and feeling, offered to get her a driver, or to give her a seat in his phaeton, which was more comfortable than her own conveyance. These proposals Bathsheba gently declined, and the farmer at once departed.

About half-an-hour later she invigorated herself by an effort, and took her seat and the reins as usual—in external appearance much as if nothing had happened.

That evening she said to Liddy, 'Wouldn't it have been different, or shouldn't I have heard more, or wouldn't they have found him, Liddy? I don't know how it is, but death would have been different from how this is. I am perfectly convinced that he is alive!'

Bathsheba remained firm in this opinion till Monday, when two circumstances conjoined to shake it. The first was a short paragraph in the local newspaper, which, beyond making presumptive evidence of Troy's death by drowning contained the important testimony of a young Mr Barker, M.D., of Budmouth who spoke to being an eyewitness of the accident in a letter to the editor.

The other circumstance was the arrival of Troy's clothes, when it became necessary for her to examine and identify them. It was so evident to her in the midst of her agitation that Troy had undressed in the full conviction of dressing again almost immediately, that the notion that anything but death could have prevented him was a perverse one to entertain.

When alone late that evening beside a small fire, Bathsheba took Troy's watch into her hand, which had been restored to her with the rest of the articles belonging to him. She opened the case. There was the little coil of pale hair which had been as the fuse to this great explosion. She took it in her hand and held it over the fire . . . 'No—I'll keep it in memory of her, poor thing!' she said snatching back her hand.

CHAPTER THIRTY-NINE

THE SHEEP FAIR

The busiest, merriest, noisiest day of the whole statute number was the day of the sheep fair. This yearly gathering was held on a level green space of ten or fifteen acres, upon the summit of a hill.

Shepherds who attended with their flocks from long distances started from home two or three days, or even a week, before the fair, driving their charges a few miles each day—not more than ten or twelve—and resting them at night in hired fields by the wayside.

The Weatherbury Farms, however, were no such long distance from the hill, and those arrangements were not necessary in their case. But the large united flocks of Bathsheba and Farmer Boldwood formed a valuable and imposing multitude which demanded much attention. On this account Gabriel, who was now Bathsheba's bailiff, in addition to Boldwood's shepherd and Cain Ball, accompanied them along the way, old George the dog of course behind them.

The great mass of sheep in the fair—bleating, panting, and weary thousands—had entered and were penned before the morning had far advanced, the dog belonging to each flock being tied to the corner of the pen containing it. Alleys for pedestrians intersected the pens, which soon became crowded with buyers and sellers from far and near.

In another part of the hill, stood a circular tent, of exceptional newness and size.

At the rear of the large tent there were two small dressing-tents. In one of these there was, sitting on the grass, pulling on a pair of jack-boots, a young man whom we instantly recognise as Sergeant Troy.

Troy's appearance in this position may be briefly accounted for. The brig aboard which he was taken in Budmouth Road was about to start on a voyage, though somewhat short of hands. Troy joined and he ultimately worked his passage to the United States, where he made a precarious living in various towns as professor of gymnastics, sword exercise, fencing, and pugilism. A few months were sufficient to give him a distaste for this kind of life.

To England he did return at last. It was with gloom he considered on landing at Liverpool that if he were to go home his reception would be of a kind very unpleasant to contemplate. Bathsheba was not a woman to be made a fool of, or a woman to suffer in silence; and how could he endure existence with a spirited wife to whom at first entering he would be beholden for food and lodging? He put off his return from day to day, and would have decided to put it off altogether if he could have found anywhere else the readymade establishment which existed for him there.

At this time he fell in with a travelling circus.

Troy was taken into the company, and a play was prepared with a view to his personation of the chief character Turpin. It was thus carelessly, and without having formed any definite plan for the future, that Troy found himself at Greenhill Fair with the rest of the company on this day.

Bathsheba—who was driven to the fair that day by Poorgrass—had, like every one else, read or heard the announcement that Mr Francis, the Great Cosmopolitan Equestrian and Roughrider, would enact the part of Turpin, and she was not yet too old and careworn to be without a little curiosity to see him. This particular show was by far the largest and grandest in the fair.

And so Bathsheba appeared in the tent. She immediately found, to her confusion, that she was the single reserved individual in the tent, the rest of the crowded spectators one and all, standing on their legs on the borders of the arena. Hence many eyes were turned upon her. Once there, Bathsheba was forced to make the best of it and remain.

Troy, on peeping from his dressing-tent through a slit before entering, saw his wife sitting as queen of the tournament. He started back in utter confusion, for although his disguise effectually concealed his personality, he instantly felt that she would be sure to recognise his voice. There arose in him a sense of shame at the possibility of being discovered by her in this mean condition. He hastily thrust aside the curtain dividing his own little dressing space from that of the manager and proprietor.

'Here's the devil to pay!' said Troy.

'How's that?'

'Why, there's a blackguard creditor in the tent I don't want to see, who'll discover me and nab me as sure as Satan if I open my mouth. Play or no play, I won't open my mouth,' said Troy firmly.

'Very well, then let me see. I tell you how we'll manage,' said the other, who perhaps felt it would be extremely awkward to offend his leading man just at this time. 'I won't tell 'em anything about your keeping silence; go on with the piece and say nothing, doing what you can by a judicious wink now and then, and a few indomitable nods in the heroic places, you know. They'll never find out that the speeches are omitted.'

This seemed feasible enough, for Turpin's speeches were not many or long, the fascination of the piece lying entirely in the action; and accordingly the play began.

Troy had added a few touches to his ordinary make-up for the character and the metamorphosis effected by judiciously 'lining' his face with a wire rendered him safe from the eyes of Bathsheba and her men. Nevertheless, he was relieved when it was got through.

There was a second performance in the evening, and the tent was lighted up. Troy had taken his part very quietly this time, venturing to introduce a few speeches on occasion; and was just concluding it when he observed within a yard of him the eye of a man darted keenly into his side features. Troy hastily shifted his position, after having recognised in the scrutineer the knavish bailiff Pennyways, his wife's sworn enemy, who still hung about the outskirts of Weatherbury.

It occurred to Troy that to find Pennyways, and make a friend of him if possible, would be a very wise act. He had put on a thick beard, and in this he wandered about the fair-field. It was now almost dark, and respectable people were getting their carts and gigs ready to go home.

Troy reached the tent door, and saw Pennyways standing among the groups there gathered. Troy glided up to him, beckoned, and whispered a few words; and with a mutual glance of concurrence the two men went into the night together.

CHAPTER FORTY

BATHSHEBA TALKS WITH HER OUTRIDER

The arrangement for getting back again to Weatherbury had been that Oak should take the place of Poorgrass in Bathsheba's conveyance and drive her home.

But having fallen in with Farmer Boldwood accidentally (on her part at least) at the refreshment-tent, she found it impossible to refuse his offer to ride on horseback beside her as escort.

She would not, on any consideration, treat Boldwood harshly, having once already ill-used him, and the moon having risen, and the gig being ready, she drove across the hill-top in the wending ways which led downwards. Boldwood mounted his horse and followed in close attendance behind. Thus they descended into the lowlands, and got upon the high road.

He soon found an excuse for advancing from his position in the rear, and rode close by her side. They had gone two or three miles in the moonlight, when Boldwood said suddenly and simply—

'Mrs Troy, you will marry again some day?'

This point-blank query unmistakably confused her, and it was not till a minute or more had elapsed that she said, 'You forget that my husband's death was never absolutely proved, and may not have taken place; so that I may not be really a widow.'

'Not absolutely proved, perhaps, but it was proved circumstantially. No reasonable person has any doubt of his death; nor have you, ma'am, I should imagine.'

'O yes I have, or I should have acted differently,' she said gently. 'From the first I have had a strange unaccountable feeling that he could not have perished. But even were I half persuaded that

I shall see him no more, I am far from thinking of marriage with another.'

They were silent now awhile. Then Boldwood said, 'I have always this dreary pleasure in thinking over those past times with you—that I was something to you before he was anything, and that you belonged almost to me. But of course, that's nothing. You never liked me.'

'I did; and respected you, too. My treatment of you was thoughtless, inexcusable, wicked! I shall eternally regret it. If there had been anything I could have done to make amends I would most gladly have done it.'

'Do you know that without further proof of any kind you may marry again in about six years from the present—subject to nobody's objection or blame?'

'O yes,' she said quickly. 'I know all that.'

'Now, listen once more,' Boldwood pleaded. 'If I wait that long, will you marry me? You own that you owe me amends—let that be your way of making them. O Bathsheba, promise—it is only a little promise—that if you marry again, you will marry me!'

His tone was so excited that she almost feared him at this moment, even whilst she sympathised. She said, with some distress in her voice. 'I will never marry another man whilst you wish me to be your wife, whatever comes—but to say more—you have taken me so by surprise.'

'But let it stand in these simple words—that in six years' time you will be my wife?'

She breathed; and then said mournfully. 'O what shall I do? I don't love you, and I much fear that I never shall love you as much as a woman ought to love her husband. If you value such an act of friendship from a woman who doesn't esteem herself as she did, and has little love left, why I—I will.'

'Promise!'

'—Consider, if I cannot promise soon.'

'But soon is perhaps never?'

'O no, it is not! I mean soon. Christmas, we'll say.'

'Christmas!' he said nothing further till he added: 'Well, I'll say no more to you about it till that time.'

CHAPTER FORTY-ONE

CONVERGING COURSES

1

Christmas-eve came, and a party that Boldwood was to give in the evening was the great subject of talk in Weatherbury. It was not that the rarity of Christmas parties in the parish made this one a wonder, but that Boldwood should be the giver. The announcement had had an abnormal and incongruous sound. That the party was intended to be a truly jovial one there was no room for doubt, but the spirit of revelry was wanting in the atmosphere of the house. Such a thing had never been attempted before by its owner, the organisation of the whole effort was carried out coldly by hirelings, and a shadow seemed to move about the rooms, saying that the proceedings were unnatural to the place and the lone man who lived therein, and hence not good.

2

Bathsheba was in her room, dressing for the event. 'Liddy,' said Bathsheba almost timidly. 'I am foolishly agitated—I cannot tell why. I wish I had not been obliged to go to this dance; but there's no escaping now. I shall make my appearance of course, but I am the cause of the party, and that upsets me! I wish I had never seen Weatherbury.'

'That's wicked of you—to wish to be worse off than you are.'

'No, Liddy. I have never been free from trouble since I have lived here, and this party is likely to bring me more. Now, fetch my black silk dress, and see how it sits upon me.'

3

Boldwood was dressing also at this hour. A tailor from Casterbridge was with him, assisting him in the operation of trying on a new coat that had just been brought home.

Never had Boldwood been so fastidious, unreasonable about the fit, and generally difficult to please. He at last expressed himself satisfied.

As Boldwood continued awhile in his room alone—ready and dressed to receive his company—the mood of anxiety about his appearance seemed to pass away, and to be succeeded by a deep solemnity. However his feverish anxiety continued to show its existence by a galloping motion of his fingers upon the side of his thigh as he went down the stairs.

4

Troy was sitting in a corner of The White Hart tavern at Casterbridge. A knock was given at the door, and Pennyways entered.

'Well, have you seen him?' Troy enquired, pointing to a chair.

'Boldwood?'

'No—Lawyer Long.'

'He wadn' at home. I went there first too.'

'Yet I don't see that, because a man appears to be drowned and was not, he should be liable for anything. I shan't ask any lawyer—not I. Now, what I want to know is this, do you think there's really anything going on between her and Boldwood?'

'I haen't been able to learn. There's a deal of feeling on his side seemingly, but I don't answer for her. She's not fond of him—quite offish and quite careless, I know.'

'I'm not too sure of that . . . she's a handsome woman, Pennyways, is she not? Own that you never saw a finer or more splendid creature in your life. Upon my honour, when I set eyes upon her that day I wondered what I could have been made of to be able to leave her by herself so long. And then I was hampered with that bothering show, which I'm free of at last, thank the stars. I must go and find her out at once—O yes, I see that—I must go.'

Troy buttoned on a heavy grey overcoat with cape and high collar, the latter being erect and rigid, like a girdling wall, and nearly reaching to the verge of a travelling cap which was pulled down over his ears.

'How does this cover me?' he said to Pennyways, 'Nobody would recognise me now, I'm sure.'

Pennyways snuffed the candle, and then looked up and deliberately inspected Troy.

'You've made up your mind to go then?' he said.

'Made up my mind? Yes; of course I have,' said Troy angrily.

'There she is with plenty of money, and a house and farm, and horses, and comfort, and here am I living from hand to mouth—a needy adventurer. Besides, it is no use talking now; it is too late, and I am glad of it; I've been seen and recognised here this very afternoon.

'Now, let me see what the time is,' he said, after emptying his glass in one draught as he stood. 'Half-past six o'clock. I shall not hurry along the road, and shall be there then before nine.'

CHAPTER FORTY-TWO

CONCURRITUR – HORAE MOMENTO*

Outside the front of Boldwood's house a group of men stood in the dark, with their faces towards the door.

'He was seen in Casterbridge this afternoon—so the boy said,' one of them remarked in a whisper. 'And I for one believe it. His body was never found, you know.'

''Tis a strange story,' said the next. 'You may depend upon't that she knows nothing about it.'

'If he's alive and here in the neighbourhood, he means mischief,' said the first. 'Poor young thing; I do pity her, if 'tis true. He'll drag her to the dogs.'

They stood silent, every man busied with his own thoughts.

'I wish we had told of the report at once,' said one of the men.

'More harm may come of this than we know of. What's to be done?'

* The title is part of a quotation from Horace's *Satires* which when translated reads as 'Battle is joined, and in a moment of time comes speedy death or joyous victory.'

'Laban, you know her best,' said Samway. 'You'd better go and ask to speak to her.'

'I bain't fit for any such thing,' said Laban, nervously. 'If 'twas to save my life, I couldn't!'

The men stood outside the house for over an hour, debating what was to be done. Then Samway said gloomily, 'I suppose we had better all go in together. Perhaps I may have a chance of saying a word to master.'

So the men entered the hall, which was the room selected and arranged for the gathering because of its size. The younger men and maids were at last just beginning a dance. Bathsheba had resolved upon staying for about an hour only, and gliding off unobserved, having from the first made up her mind that she could on no account dance, sing, or take any active part in the proceedings.

Her allotted hour having been passed in chatting and looking on, Bathsheba told Liddy not to hurry herself, and went to the small parlour to prepare for departure.

Nobody was in the room, but she had hardly been there a moment when the master of the house entered.

'Mrs Troy—you are not going?' he said. 'We've hardly begun!'

'If you'll excuse me, I should like to go now.'

'I've been trying to get an opportunity of speaking to you,' said Boldwood. 'You know perhaps what I long to say?'

Bathsheba silently looked on the floor.

'You do give it?' he said, eagerly.

'What?' she whispered.

'Now, that's evasion! Why, the promise. A promise to marry me at the end of five years and three-quarters. You owe it to me!'

'I feel that I do,' said Bathsheba; 'that is, if you demand it.'

'You'll marry me between five and six years hence?'

'Don't press me too hard. I'll marry nobody else.'

'But surely you will name the time, or there's nothing in the promise at all? Promise yourself to me; I deserve it, indeed it do, for I have loved you more than anybody in the world! And if I said hasty words and showed uncalled for heat of manner towards you, believe me, dear, I did not mean to distress you; I was in agony, Bathsheba, and I did not know what I said. You wouldn't let a dog suffer what I have suffered, could you but know it! Sometimes

I shrink from your knowing what I have felt for you, and sometimes I am distressed that all of it you never will know. Be gracious and give up a little to me, when I would give up my life for you!'

The trimmings of her dress, as they quivered against the light, showed how agitated she was, and at last she burst out crying. 'And you'll not—press me—about anything more—if I say in five or six years?' she sobbed, when she had power to frame the words.

'Yes, then I'll leave it to time.'

'Very well. If he does not return, I'll marry you in six years from this day, if we both live,' she said solemnly.

Boldwood pressed her hand. 'I am happy now,' he said, 'God bless you!'

He left the room. Bathsheba cloaked the effects of the late scene as she best could, and in a few moments came downstairs with her hat and cloak on, ready to go. To get to the door it was necessary to pass through the hall, and before doing to she paused on the bottom of the staircase which descended into one corner, to take a last look at the gathering.

There was no music or dancing in progress just now. At the lower end, which had been arranged for the work-folk specially, a group conversed in whispers, and with clouded looks. Boldwood was standing by the fireplace, and he had observed their peculiar manner, and their looks askance.

'What is it you are in doubt about, men?' he said.

One of them turned and replied uneasily; 'It was something Laban heard of, that's all, sir.'

'Mrs Troy has come downstairs,' said Samway to Tall. 'If you want to tell her, you had better do it now.'

'Do you know what they mean?' the farmer asked Bathsheba, across the room.

'I don't in the least,' said Bathsheba.

There was a smart rapping at the door. One of the men opened it instantly, and went outside.

'Mrs Troy is wanted,' he said, on returning.

'Quite ready,' said Bathsheba. 'Though I didn't tell them to send.'

'It is a stranger, ma'am,' said the man by the door.

'A stranger?' she said.

'Ask him to come in,' said Boldwood.

The message was given, and Troy, wrapped up to his eyes as we have seen him stood in the doorway.

There was an unearthly silence, all looking towards the newcomer. Those who had just learnt that he was in the neighbourhood recognised him instantly; those who did not were perplexed.

Boldwood was among those who did not notice that he was Troy. 'Come in, come in,' he repeated cheerfully, 'and drain a Christmas beaker with us, stranger!'

Troy next advanced into the middle of the room, took off his cap, turned down his coat-collar, and looked Boldwood in the face. Troy began to laugh a mechanical laugh; Boldwood recognised him now.

Troy turned to Bathsheba. The poor girl's wretchedness at this time was beyond all fancy or narration. She had sunk down on the lowest stair; and there she sat, her mouth blue and dry, and her dark eyes fixed vacantly upon him.

Then Troy spoke. 'Bathsheba, I come here for you!'

She made no reply.

'Come home with me; come!'

Bathsheba moved her feet a little, but did not rise.

Troy went across to her.

'Come, madam, do you hear what I say?' he said peremptorily.

A strange voice came from the fireplace. Hardly a soul in the assembly recognised the thin tones to be those of Boldwood. Sudden despair had transformed him.

'Bathsheba, go with your husband!'

Nevertheless, she did not move. The truth was that Bathsheba was beyond the pale of activity—and yet not in a swoon.

Troy stretched out his hand to pull her towards him, when she quickly shrank back. This visible dread of him seemed to irritate Troy, and he seized her arm and pulled it sharply. At the moment of his seizure she writhed, and gave a quick, low scream.

The scream had been heard but a few seconds when it was followed by a sudden deafening report that echoed through the room and stupefied them all.

In bewilderment they turned their eyes to Boldwood. At his back, as he stood before the fireplace, was a gun-rack, as is usual in farmhouses, constructed to hold two guns. 'When Bathsheba had cried out in her husband's grasp, Boldwood's face of gnashing despair had changed. He had turned quickly, taken one of the guns, cocked it, and at once discharged it at Troy.

Troy fell. He uttered a long guttural sigh—there was a contraction—an extension—then his muscles relaxed, and he lay still.

Boldwood was seen through the smoke to be now in the act of turning the second barrel upon himself. Samway his man was the first to see this, and in the midst of the general horror darted up to him. The gun exploded a second time, sending its contents by a timely blow from Samway, into the beam which crossed the ceiling.

'Well, it makes no difference!' Boldwood gasped. 'There is another way for me to die.'

Then he broke away from Samway, crossed the room to Bathsheba, and kissed her hand. He put on his hat, opened the door, and went into the darkness, nobody thinking of preventing him.

CHAPTER FORTY-THREE

AFTER THE SHOCK

Boldwood passed into the high road, turned in the direction of Casterbridge, and between eleven and twelve o'clock crossed the moor into the town. He halted before an archway of heavy stonework, which was closed by an iron-studded pair of doors. This was the entrance to the goal, and over it a lamp was fixed, the light enabling the wretched traveller to find a bell-pull.

The small wicket at last opened, and a porter appeared. Boldwood stepped forward, and said something in a low tone. Another man came. Boldwood entered, and the door was closed behind him, and he walked the world no more.

Long before this time Weatherbury had been thoroughly aroused. Oak was one of the first to hear of the catastrophe, and when he entered the room Bathsheba was sitting on the floor beside the body of Troy, his head pillowed in her lap. The temporary coma had ceased and activity had come with the necessity for it. Bathsheba was astonishing all around her now. She was of the stuff of which great men's mothers are made.

'Gabriel,' she said automatically, when he entered, 'Ride to Casterbridge instantly for a surgeon. It is, I believe, useless, but go. Mr Boldwood has shot my husband.'

The miles necessary to be traversed, and other hindrances delayed the arrival of Mr Aldritch the surgeon; and more than three hours passed between the time at which the shot was fired and that of his entering the house. Having hastened into the hall he found it in darkness and quite deserted. He drove at once to Bathsheba's.

The first person he met was Liddy.

'What has been done?' he said.

'I don't know, sir,' said Liddy with suspended breath. 'My mistress has done it all.'

They went upstairs together. Liddy knocked, and Bathsheba's dress was heard rustling across the room: the key turned in the lock, and she opened the door.

'Oh, Mr Aldritch, you have come at last,' she murmured, and threw back the door. 'Well, all is done, and anybody in the world may see him now.' She then passed by him and entered another room.

The doctor went in. 'It is all done, indeed, as she says,' he remarked in a subdued voice. 'The body has been undressed and properly laid out in grave clothes. Gracious Heaven—this mere girl! She must have the nerve of a stoic.'

'The heart of a wife merely,' floated in a whisper, and turning he saw Bathsheba. Then, as if to prove that her fortitude had been more of will than of spontaneity, she silently sank down on the floor.

The medical attention which had been useless in Troy's case was invaluable in Bathsheba's, who fell into a series of fainting fits that had a serious aspect for a time. Liddy kept watch in Bathsheba's chamber, where she heard her mistress moaning in whispers through the dull slow hours of that wretched night: 'O it is my fault—how can I live!'

CHAPTER FORTY-FOUR

THE MARCH FOLLOWING—BATHSHEBA BOLDWOOD

We pass rapidly on into the month of March. A discovery was made throwing more light on Boldwood's conduct and condition than any details which had preceded it.

That he had been from the time of Greenhill Fair until the fatal Christmas Eve in excited and unusual moods was known to those who had been intimate with him; but nobody imagined the mental derangement which Bathsheba alone had momentarily suspected. In a locked closet was now discovered an extraordinary collection of articles. There were several sets of ladies' dresses all of colours which from Bathsheba's style of dress might have been judged to be her favourites. There were two muffs, sable and ermine. Above all there was a case of jewellery containing four heavy gold bracelets and several lockets and rings. They were all carefully packed in paper, and each package was labelled 'Bathsheba Boldwood', a date being subjoined six years in advance in every instance.

This somewhat pathetic evidence of a mind crazed with love was the subject of discourse in Warren's malthouse when Oak entered from Casterbridge with tidings of the sentence, and his face told the tale sufficiently well. Boldwood, as everyone supposed he would do, had pleaded guilty, and had been sentenced to death.

The conviction that Boldwood had not been morally responsible for his later acts now became general. A petition was addressed to the Home Secretary, advancing the circumstances which appeared to justify a request for a reconsideration of the sentence.

The upshot of the petition was waited for in Weatherbury with solicitous interest. The execution had been fixed for a Saturday morning about a fortnight after the sentence was passed, and up to Friday afternoon no answer had been received. At that time Gabriel came from Casterbridge Gaol, whither he had been to wish Boldwood goodbye.

It was dark when he reached home and half the village was out to meet him.

'No tidings,' Gabriel said wearily. 'And I'm afraid there's no hope. Has there been any change in our mistress this afternoon?'

'None at all. She keeps on asking if you be come and if there's news.'

'Laban is here, isn't he?' said Oak.

'Yes,' said Tall.

'What I've arranged is, that you shall ride to town the last thing tonight; leave here about nine, and wait a while there, getting about twelve. If nothing has been received by eleven to-night, they say there's no chance at all.'

'I do so hope his life will be spared,' said Liddy. 'If it is not, she'll go out of her mind too. Poor thing; her sufferings have been dreadful; she deserves anybody's pity. If you haven't seen poor mistress since Christmas you wouldn't know her. Her eyes are so miserable that she's not the same woman.'

Laban departed as directed, and at eleven o'clock that night several of the villagers strolled along the road to Casterbridge and awaited his arrival—among them Oak, and nearly all the rest of Bathsheba's men. Gabriel's anxiety was great that Boldwood might be saved, even though in his conscience he felt that he ought to die, for there had been qualities in the farmer which Oak loved. At last, when they were all weary the tramp of a horse was heard.

'Is that you, Laban?' said Gabriel.

'Yes—'tis come. He's not to die. 'Tis confinement during Her Majesty's pleasure.'

'Hurrah!' said Coggan, with a swelling heart. 'God's above the devil yet!'

CHAPTER FORTY-FIVE

BEAUTY IN LONELINESS – AFTER ALL

Bathsheba revived with the spring. But she remained alone now for the greater part of her time, and stayed in the house. She shunned every one, even Liddy, and could be brought to make no confidences, and to ask for no sympathy.

As the summer drew on she passed more of her time in the open air, and began to examine into farming matters from sheer necessity, though she never rode out. One Friday evening in August she walked a little way along the road and entered the village for the first time since the sombre event of the preceding Christmas. None of the old colour had as yet come to her cheek, and its absolute paleness was heightened by the jet black of her gown, till it appeared preternatural. Her stealthy walk was to the nook where Fanny Robin's grave lay, and she came to the marble tombstone.

A motion of satisfaction enlivened her face as she read the complete inscription. First came the words of Troy himself:—

ERECTED BY FRANCIS TROY
IN BELOVED MEMORY OF
FANNY ROBIN,
WHO DIED OCTOBER 9TH, 18—, AGED 20 YEARS.

Underneath this was now inscribed in new letters:—

IN THE SAME GRAVE LIE
THE REMAINS OF THE AFORESAID
FRANCIS TROY
WHO DIED DECEMBER 24TH, 18—, AGED 26 YEARS.

Whilst she stood and read and meditated, Bathsheba did not notice a form which came up quietly and on seeing her, first moved as if to retreat, then paused and regarded her. Bathsheba did not raise her head for some time, and when she looked round her face was wet, and her eyes drowned and dim. 'Mr Oak,' exclaimed she, disconcerted, 'how long have you been here?'

'A few minutes, ma'am,' said Oak, respectfully. 'Were you going into church?'

'No,' she said, 'I came to see the tombstone privately—to see if they had cut the inscription as I wished.'

'And have they done it as you wished?' said Oak.

'Yes. And now I am going home, Mr Oak.'

Oak walked after her. 'I wanted to name a small matter to you as soon as I could,' he said with hesitation. 'Merely about business, and I think I may just mention it now, if you'll allow me.'

'O yes, certainly.'

'It is that I may soon have to give up the management of your farm, Mrs Troy. The fact is, I am thinking of leaving England—not yet, you know—next spring.'

'Leaving England!' she said, in surprise and genuine disappointment. 'Why, Gabriel, what are you going to do that for?'

'Well, I've thought it best,' Oak stammered out. 'California is the spot I've had in my mind to try.'

'But it is understood everwhere that you are going to take poor Mr Boldwood's farm on your own account?'

'Nothing is settled yet, and I have reasons for giving up.'

'And what shall I do without you? Oh, Gabriel, I don't think you ought to go away. You've been with me so long—through bright times and dark times—such old friends as we are—that it seems unkind almost. I had fancied that if you leased the other farm as master, you might still give a helping look across at mine. Yet now that I am more helpless than ever you go away!'

'Yes, that's the ill fortune o'it,' said Gabriel, in a distressed tone. 'And it is because of that very helplessness that I feel bound to go. Good afternoon, ma'am,' he concluded, in evident anxiety to get away, and at once went out by a path she could follow on no pretence whatever.

Bathsheba went home, her mind occupied with a new trouble. He who had believed in her and argued on her side when all the rest of the world was against her, had at last like the others become weary and neglectful of the old cause, and was leaving her to fight her battles alone.

The autumn wore away gloomily enough and Christmas-day came, completing a year of her legal widowhood, and two years and a quarter of her life alone. The next morning brought a formal notice by letter from Oak that he should not renew his engagement with her for the following Lady-day.

So desolate was Bathsheba that evening, that in an absolute hunger for pity and sympathy, and miserable in that she appeared to have outlived the only true friendship she had ever owned, she went down to Oak's house just after sunset.

A lively firelight shone from the window, but nobody was visible in the room. She tapped nervously, and then thought it doubtful if it were right for a single woman to call upon a bachelor who lived alone, although he was her manager, and she might be supposed to call on business without any real impropriety. Gabriel opened the door, and the moon shone upon his forehead.

'Mr Oak,' said Bathsheba faintly.

'Yes; I am Mr Oak,' said Gabriel. 'Who have I the honour—O how stupid of me, not to know you, mistress!'

'I shall not be your mistress much longer, shall I, Gabriel?' she said in pathetic tones.

'Well, no. I suppose—But come in, ma'am. Will you sit down, please? Here's a chair.'

So down she sat, and down he sat, the fire dancing in their faces.

'You'll think it strange that I have come, but—'

'O no; not at all.'

'But I thought—Gabriel, I have been uneasy in the belief that I have offended you, and that you are going away on that account. It grieved me very much, and I couldn't help coming.'

'Offended me! As if you could do that, Bathsheba!'

'Haven't I?' she asked, gladly. 'But, what are you going away for else?'

'I am not going to emigrate, you know; I wasn't aware that you would wish me not to when I told 'ee, or I shouldn't have thought of doing it,' he said, simply. 'Nothing would prevent my attending to your business as before, hadn't it been that things have been said about us.'

'What?' said Bathsheba in surprise. 'Things said about you and me! What are they?'

'The top and tail o't is this—that I'm sniffing about here, and waiting for poor Boldwood's farm, with a thought of getting you some day.'

'Getting me! What does that mean?'

'Marrying of 'ee, in plain British. You asked me to tell, so you mustn't blame me.'

Bathsheba did not look quite so alarmed as if a cannon had been discharged by her ear, which was what Oak had expected.

'Marrying me! I didn't know it was that you meant,' she said, quietly.

Gabriel looked her long in the face, but the firelight being faint there was not much to be seen. 'Bathsheba,' he said, tenderly and in surprise, and coming closer. 'If I only knew one thing—whether you would allow me to love you and win you, and marry you after all—If I only knew that!'

'But you never will know,' she murmured.

'Why?'

'Because you never ask.'

'Oh—Oh!' said Gabriel, with a low laugh of joyousness. 'My own dear—You know that I, as an unmarried man, carrying on a business for you as a very taking young woman, had a proper hard part to play—more particular that people knew I had a sort of feeling for 'ee; and I fancied, from the way we were mentioned together, that it might injure your good name. Nobody knows the heat and fret I have been caused by it.'

'O, how glad I am I came!' she exclaimed, thankfully, as she rose from her seat. 'I have thought so much more of you since I fancied you did not want even to see me again. But I must be going now, or I shall be missed. Why, Gabriel,' she said, with a slight laugh, as they went to the door, 'it seems exactly as if I had come courting you—how dreadful!'

'And quite right, too,' said Oak, 'I've danced at your skittish heels, my beautiful Bathsheba, for many a long mile, and many a long day; and it is hard to begrudge me this one visit.'

He accompanied her up the hill. They spoke very little of their mutual feelings; pretty phrases and warm expressions being probably unnecessary between such tried friends. Theirs was that substantial affection which arises (if any arises at all) when the two who are thrown together begin first by knowing the rougher sides of each other's character, and not the best till further on, the romance growing up in the interstices of a mass of hard prosaic reality. This good-fellowship—camaraderie—usually occurring through similarity of pursuits, is unfortunately seldom superadded to love between the sexes, because men and women associate, not in their labours, but in their pleasures merely. Where, however, happy circumstance permits its development, the compounded feeling proves itself to be the only love which is strong as death—that love which many waters cannot quench, nor the floods drown, beside which the passion usually called by the name is evanescent as steam.

SUMMARIES, GLOSSARY AND COMPREHENSION

Chapter 1

Summary

Farmer Gabriel Oak was a twenty-eight year old bachelor of likeable and impressive appearance and character. He dressed casually, was humble, unassuming, and ill at ease even in his Sunday 'best'. He was mature and of sound judgment. While in the fields at Norcombe Hill, Oak saw a colourful spring wagon coming down the ridge. The waggoner walked alongside and a young, attractive girl sat on the top of the wagon. The waggoner announced that the tailboard had fallen off and leaving the wagon there, returned to retrieve it. The girl in the meantime took out a mirror and gazed at herself unselfconsciously. When they reached the turnpike gate, she refused to pay the two pence needed to complete the toll. Oak paid the amount. The wagon passed. Oak wondered at the vanity of the girl. She was beautiful; she was also proud. Oak was fascinated by her.

Glossary

'When Farmer Oak smiled, the corners of his mouth spread . . . appeared round them'	a detailed, humorous description of Gabriel Oak's smile.
chinks	small openings
misty	indistinct
hampered	hindered
high winds	strong gusty winds
Dr Johnson	Dr Samuel Johnson (1709–83) was a great English writer. He was known to wear a coat which was so huge that his books could be carried in the pockets

lower extremities	legs
leggings	protective over-garment for the legs worn from knee to ankle
hues and curves had tarried on to manhood	the typical colour and softness associated with teenagers as contrasted with the fully developed adult body. In Oak, they still remained.
relics	remains
unassumingly	modestly
apex	highest part of the wagon
tailboard	a hinged flap at the back of a wagon which may be lowered for loading or unloading
turnpike gate	a gate made of pikes set across a main road or highway to stop vehicles for the payment of toll, used for upkeep of roads
disputants	those quarrelling or arguing
handsome	attractive
piqued	displeased and hurt
comely	attractive

Comprehension

1. What is the aspect of Gabriel Oak's personality referred to in the opening sentence? What is it about the choice of words that makes the description effective?
2. Oak was a different man on working days and on Sundays. What was the difference and what caused it?
3. How does Hardy give us an idea of Oak's age and appearance? Describe Gabriel Oak in your own words.
4. 'She simply observed herself as a fair product of Nature'. What was the girl engaged in doing when the waggoner was away? What does this say of her?
5. What happened at the toll-gate? What did Oak do? What does this say of him?
6. How did the girl respond to his gesture? How does it set the tone of the story? What is one led to expect?

7. What is striking about the opening chapter of the novel in terms of description and narration?

CHAPTER 2

SUMMARY

Farmer Oak played his flute even as he kept vigil in his shepherd's hut during the lambing season. Oak had been a shepherd, then a bailiff, and only lately had become a farmer. He had leased a small sheep farm stocked with two hundred sheep. Oak was passing through a critical juncture on account of this financial commitment. It was the lambing season and Farmer Oak also oversaw the birth of the lambs. He brought a newborn lamb indoors and placed it on a wisp of hay before the stove. He fell asleep immediately on his hard couch made up of corn sacks.

GLOSSARY

St Thomas's eve	20/ 21st December in English folklore
lambing season	season when ewes give birth to lambs
latterly	recently
chronic	lasting a long time, especially illness
extinguished	put out
bailiff	the paid manager of the farm
hireling	person employed to do menial work
speck	tiny spot (referring to the newborn lamb)
wisp	a small bunch (of hay)

COMPREHENSION

1. Describe the shepherd's hut and the way it was constructed. What was its special feature that was useful?
2. What was the venture that Oak undertook without help? Explain why it was so critical.

3. How does the author communicate to the reader the fact that Oak was ambitious and hardworking?
4. What is referred to in the chapter as 'lambing of ewes'?
5. Why did Oak perform this task himself and not with the help of a hireling? Comment on Gabriel Oak's character.

CHAPTER 3

SUMMARY

At daybreak Oak saw the woman who owed him twopence, riding elegantly on an auburn pony. She was not wearing a riding habit, nor did she have a side-saddle. Oak was amused and amazed to see her ride so dexterously through the rich foliage, lying flat on the pony's back with her feet against its shoulders. Next she sat astride the pony like a man, unaware that there was an onlooker. After some days the freeze set in and Gabriel Oak heaped more fuel in his fire inside the hut to keep himself warm; however, he forgot to keep the ventilating holes open at night before falling asleep. His dog which nearly suffocated howled and someone came to save him. Oak was immensely grateful to the woman who saved his life. In the conversation that followed, she refused to divulge her name. She teased him and went her way. He realised that it was the same woman who had been on the wagon earlier, and later on the horse.

GLOSSARY

sluggish	slow-moving
auburn	reddish brown
riding habit	riding attire
dexterously	skilfully
lank	thin and tall
amble	to walk at a slow relaxed pace
side-saddle	saddle in which rider has both feet on the same side of the horse (used by women riders wearing skirts)

ventilating holes	holes which allow fresh air to enter
thatched hurdle	A hurdle is a movable rectangular frame strengthened with wooden bars. Hurdles can be used to construct a temporary fence to prevent sheep from straying. When covered with straw or reeds (thatched) they form a temporary shelter.

Comprehension

1. How do men and women differ in their riding postures? What made the young lady adopt the riding postures mentioned in the text?
2. Why did she take the precaution to ensure that there was no onlooker?
3. Why did the dog howl? What accounted for the unconscious state in which Gabriel Oak was found?
4. How did the girl rescue Gabriel?
5. On hearing Oak's name the girl says, 'You seem fond of yours in speaking it so decisively, Gabriel Oak.' What does she mean?
6. Comment on the conversation and the attitude of the speakers, Gabriel Oak and the girl.

Chapter 4

Summary

Gabriel Oak was resolved that he would make Bathsheba Everdene his wife – he was so taken up with her. A golden opportunity to visit her came when a ewe died. The lamb was without succour and Oak decided to gift it to Bathsheba. When he went to her aunt, Mrs Hurst's house, Bathsheba was away. He told Mrs Hurst of his intention to marry her and was informed that she had many suitors. Gabriel left disappointed but in a matter-of-fact way. Bathsheba who had heard everything from her aunt followed him to tell him that she did not have anyone courting her. Oak tried to persuade her to marry him but she was adamant in her refusal. She did not love Gabriel Oak and she thought it was ridiculous being asked to accept a marriage proposal under such circumstances. Oak decided not to persist in this.

Glossary

stalked	pursued stealthily
an everyday sort of man	an ordinary man
exertions	effort
eel	a kind of fish which is difficult to hold
snug	comfortable
palliative	something which lessens pain
luminous	bright
disconcerted	upset
hauteur	proud haughtiness of manner
disdainfully	from feelings of pride or superiority
crabbed	bad-tempered
skittishness	silliness, lacking seriousness

Comprehension

1. What was Gabriel Oak's resolve after meeting Bathsheba? What do you think of him?
2. What were Oak's intentions in visiting Bathsheba? What gift did he take?
3. Summarise the conversation between Gabriel Oak and Mrs Hurst. What impression do you get of Mrs Hurst and of Oak?
4. Why did Bathsheba run after Gabriel Oak?
5. Give an account of the conversation between Oak and Bathsheba. How does Oak recommend himself to Bathsheba? Why does Bathsheba refuse him?

6. '. . . I shouldn't mind being a bride at a wedding, if I could be one without having a husband,' says Bathsheba to Oak. What does this statement say of her?
7. What was Gabriel Oak's final resolve?
8. Pick out instances of humour in situation and style in this chapter.
9. How does this chapter help in building the plot of the novel?

Chapter 5

Summary

Gabriel Oak learnt that Bathsheba had left for Weatherbury. He could not find out whether it was only a visit or a permanent stay. His occupation kept him busy. Of his two dogs, the older was clever and trustworthy, the younger was still learning to tend the sheep. One night Oak returned home and called to his dogs. Only one responded. Gabriel Oak went indoors to sleep and was woken up by the sheep bell tinkling with unusual urgency. Oak ran out and ascended the hill and found two hundred of his sheep missing. There was no response to his call. To his dismay he found that the sheep had fallen down the chalk pit and lay dead. The younger dog had driven the flock over the edge. Oak felt pity for his flock first before it dawned on him that he had lost everything and would never become an independent farmer. He thanked his stars that he was not married. With whatever work he put his hand to, he could clear his debt and be a free man.

Glossary

rudiments	fundamentals
insuperable	unsurmountable
brow	the summit of a hill
velocity	speed
forward ewes	ewes about to give birth to lambs
precipice	steep cliff
mangled	crushed
frugal	economical

Comprehension

1. Where had Bathsheba gone?
2. What is the tragedy described in this chapter? How did it come about?
3. How did Oak respond to it? What is his initial reaction?
4. Do you think Oak could have averted the tragedy?
5. What aspects of Oak's character are revealed in this chapter?
6. Give examples of Hardy's descriptive language in this chapter.

Chapter 6

Summary

For two months Gabriel remained unemployed. He heard of the hiring fair at Casterbridge and decided to try his luck there. Since only shepherds seemed to be in demand rather than bailiffs, he bought a shepherd's frock and crook and made himself available but no one hired him. Tired but calm, Gabriel took out his flute and played it cheerfully. He earned a small amount of money from this exercise. Hearing there was a fair at Shottsford near Weatherbury the following day, Gabriel decided to go there. He would spend the night at Weatherbury on his way to Shottsford. There he saw a hayrick on fire and made every effort to put it out. The panic-stricken labourers were directed by him resourcefully and the fire was brought under control. A young woman on horseback, the farmer of the place, stood by watching anxiously. Impressed with Gabriel Oak's endeavours to save the hayrick, she sent her maid to the 'stranger' to thank him for his service. Gabriel Oak advanced in humility, tired, covered in soot and dust, and found himself face to face with Bathsheba Everdene.

Glossary

blithe	gay
carters	drivers of carts

thatchers	men who thatch roofs, that is, cover or repair
meditative	thoughtful
shepherd's crook	the hooked staff of a shepherd
nailed up his colours	displayed his preference
'Jockey to the Fair'	an eighteenth-century folk song
preclude	make impossible, prevent from happening
clambered	climb in an awkward and laborious way
conflagration	fire
kerb	a line of raised stones separating footpath from road
smudged	blotted
grimy	covered with dirt or grime

Comprehension

1. After being unemployed for two months, what did Gabriel Oak do?
2. How would you describe Oak's frame of mind at this point?
3. In looking for work at the Casterbridge hiring fair, which group did Oak identify himself with?
4. What took him from Casterbridge to Weatherbury?
5. Describe the fire incident and the role played by Oak in putting out the fire.
6. What does this incident lead him to? What is the unexpected encounter referred to in this chapter?
7. How did Bathsheba Everdene come to be the farmer of the place?

Chapter 7

Summary

An awkwardness characterised the meeting of Bathsheba and Gabriel Oak. He was up for hire and she was willing to hire him as a shepherd. She handed him over to the bailiff to look to the practical details of hiring and left. Oak wondered at the new development that an inexperienced girl like Bathsheba had now assumed the stature of mistress of the farm. Heading for Warren's Malthouse to look for a place to stay, Oak crossed the village churchyard. There he met a timid young girl standing beside a tree. Gabriel Oak asked her for directions to Warren's Malthouse. She seemed highly excited and made him promise that he would not speak about having seen her. Noting her condition Oak offered her a shilling which she accepted. Gabriel Oak left her there and proceeded to the village of Weatherbury.

Glossary

singularity	uniqueness
conviction breeds conviction	strong belief generates the same in those around
straggled	moving slowly so as to be some distance behind the people in front
encounter	meeting
timorously	fearfully
cadence	regular beat of sound
'It suggested a consumption . . . was already too little'	The girl was highly excited and her pulse was beating rapidly. It was too much for so small a frame to bear.
Warren's Malthouse	Owned by Warren, it is a place where barley or other grain is prepared for brewing or distilling into beer, ale and the like. A malthouse was a characteristic feature of a parish, it being a place for farmhands to meet, gossip, eat and drink.

Comprehension

1. Describe Bathsheba's feelings on recognising Gabriel Oak.
2. What were Oak's reactions to the meeting?

3. 'But some women only require an emergency to make them fit for one.' What is being referred to here?
4. Describe the girl Oak met on the way to the malthouse. What are your impressions about the girl and her state of mind?
5. How did Gabriel Oak help her? What does this gesture say of Oak?

Chapter 8

Summary

The malthouse was a simple but cheerful place. Gabriel Oak's entry was greeted by warmth and friendliness of the part of the rustics. In an atmosphere pervaded by the sweet smell of new malt, the camaraderie was striking. The shepherds spoke about Bathsheba and her deceased parents. Gabriel was asked to play his flute to entertain them. He was to lodge with Jan Coggan. News came that Bathsheba had sacked her bailiff for stealing barley. Also the news that Fanny Robin, Bathsheba's youngest servant, was missing. The search would be on. Bathsheba showed her concern by inviting the farmhands to speak to them on the matter. She was informed that Fanny was secretive concerning her relationship with a soldier, with whom she might have gone away.

Glossary

skimmed	passed over, lightly touched
gnarled	twisted with age
magnanimously	generously
neck and crop	headlong
bailey	bailiff
'fleed at'	flew at
maltster	a maker of malt
casement	a window
'She was very close about it'	She was very secretive about it.

'The delight of merely seeing her . . . between seeing and possessing'	Gabriel Oak was delighted to see Bathsheba. It was a joy that wiped away the distinction between just seeing her and making her his own.

Comprehension

1. Describe the malthouse highlighting its salient features.
2. Attempt an appreciation of the manner in which the rustics are presented and their conversation portrayed.
3. How was Oak received by the rustics?
4. 'Gabriel's bosom thrilled gently as he thus slipped under the notice of the assembly the innermost subject of his heart.' What does the 'subject' refer to?
5. What was the news brought by Henry Fray first, and Susan Tall's husband, next?
6. How did Bathsheba respond to the news concerning Fanny Robin?
7. What occupied Gabriel Oak's thoughts as he lay down to sleep?

Summary

Bathsheba with the help of Liddy her servant-companion, was sorting out the belongings of her late uncle in one of the upper rooms. She was informed that there was a visitor. Not being in a presentable state, Bathsheba refused to see him. She was told that the visitor was Mr Boldwood, a gentleman-farmer who was a bachelor. He had come to get information about the missing Fanny Robin whom he had looked after since childhood till she joined Bathsheba's uncle's farm. Liddy went on to make small talk with Bathsheba concerning possible suitors. The farmhands put an end to Liddy's chatter as they came in to collect their wages.

Glossary

homestead	a farm with its buildings
bower	country cottage
hoary	greyish
Classic Renaissance	the period from mid-sixteenth to early seventeenth century when there was a revival of classical forms of art and architecture
naturalised	to become a native of a new place
Philistines	The Philistines harassed the Israelites; the term is used to refer to someone uncultured and with material interests.

Comprehension

1. What engaged the attention of Bathsheba and her helper, Liddy, in the house?
2. Who was the visitor? Why did Bathsheba refuse to meet him?
3. What was the purpose of Mr Boldwood's visit? What kind of man was he?
4. Mr Boldwood is seen through the eyes of Liddy. How does this affect the portrayal?
5. Why are the rustics called 'Philistines'?

Chapter 10

Summary

Bathsheba paid her employees as per the time-book and informed them that she had dismissed the bailiff for thieving. She had decided to do the work herself and there would be no replacement. Cainy Ball was appointed as under-shepherd to Gabriel Oak. William Smallbury who had been sent to Casterbridge on an errand brought the news that Fanny Robin had run away with the soldiers, in search of her lover. Bathsheba sent a messenger to inform Farmer Boldwood as much.

Glossary

audible	heard
time book	book in which workmen's hours are recorded
surged	moved suddenly

Comprehension

1. Describe Bathsheba's first meeting with her farm workers.
2. How did she deal with them? How did they react to her?
3. What qualities of Bathsheba as a person and as an employer are revealed in this chapter?
4. What news was received about Fanny Robin? How did Bathsheba deal with the news?
5. What were Gabriel Oak's reactions to the news and his conclusions?
6. Give an account of the rustics and their behaviour. Show how they contribute to the humour in the novel.

Chapter 11

Summary

Bathsheba's first public appearance as a farmer was in the cornmarket at Casterbridge. Attractive and elegantly dressed she drew the attention of the farmers there. The only person who seemed unmoved by her presence was a man of great dignity, perhaps between the ages of thirty-five and fifty—Mr Boldwood. Bathsheba noticed him, his appearance and his attitude. He seemed to have aroused her interest.

Glossary

by proxy no more	not having to represent someone
thronged	densely packed

Corn Exchange	The exchange and trade of grain was done in a large building, the corn market.
lumbering dialogues	slow, heavy manner of speaking
thrown into greater relief	became very noticeable
piqued	felt slighted
unimpeachable	blameless
gig	a light carriage with two wheels, drawn by one horse

COMPREHENSION

1. What is the Corn Exchange?
2. Describe Bathsheba at the cornmarket. Why did she attract attention?
3. Who was the 'black sheep' ? Why is he so called?
4. How does the author describe this man who stands out from the others?
5. Why did Bathsheba find him interesting?
6. What are Bathsheba's observations of the morning at the Corn Exchange? How does Liddy respond?
7. Comment on Bathsheba's friendship with Liddy. (Use information from the earlier chapters as well to answer this question.)

CHAPTER 12

SUMMARY

Bathsheba and Liddy were together after dinner on a Sunday. Liddy pointed out that while at church Mr Boldwood never even looked at her. It was Valentine's Eve and Bathsheba had bought a gorgeous card for young Teddy Coggan. Liddy mischievously wondered what it would be like to send the card to Mr Boldwood. Bathsheba who felt slighted by Mr Boldwood's indifference and the fact that Liddy had noticed it, decided to send him the valentine's card with the words, 'Marry me.'

Glossary

valentine	14 February, celebrated as Lovers' Day in which cards are sent, often in jest, to members of the opposite sex
nettled	stung
abstruse	confused
embossed	pressed on the reverse to create a raised ornamental pattern
irrepressible	uncontrollable
rather harassing than piquant	rather worrying than hurting
serenity	calmness
frolicsomely	playfully

Comprehension

1. Liddy is compared to a shallow brook. What does this say of her? Why does Bathsheba seek out her company?
2. What was Liddy's piece of gossip concerning Mr Boldwood in church? How did Bathsheba react?
3. What is a valentine? For whom had Bathsheba bought one?
4. What was Liddy's suggestion regarding the valentine and Boldwood?
5. How did Bathsheba and Liddy arrive at the decision concerning the valentine card?
6. What was the message on the seal?
7. What do you think of Bathsheba's action?

Chapter 13

Summary

The valentine made a deep impression on Boldwood. He did not realise it was a playful missive. His imagination ran riot as he wondered who the woman was who had sent it, and was haunted by a vision of her appearance. Another letter was delivered but it was for the new shepherd engaged by Bathsheba. Boldwood who had opened it by mistake decided to deliver it to Oak himself.

GLOSSARY

mantelshelf	shelf above a fireplace
missive	letter
symmetry	balance
impertinence	rudeness

COMPREHENSION

1. Give an account of Boldwood's reaction to the valentine. Is it justified?
2. What vision did he have of the woman who had sent it? What does Boldwood's reaction say of his nature?
3. What did Boldwood expect when he went out?
4. What did he mistakenly do on receiving a second envelope?
5. What did he decide to do with it, and why?

CHAPTER 14

SUMMARY

The carters, waggoners, and other rustics gathered at the malthouse. They felt that Bathsheba would regret the dismissal of Pennyways the bailiff. Gabriel Oak entered with newborn lambs and deposited them near the fire. He thanked the maltster for allowing him to do this as there was no lambing hut like the one he had at Norcombe. Boldwood came in to give Gabriel Oak his letter. The letter was from Fanny Robin who had written to thank Oak for his kindness to her, a stranger. The letter also informed him that her marriage to Sergeant Troy of the 11th Dragoon Guards would soon take place and that they would visit Weatherbury. Boldwood was not pleased with this news. He did not trust Sergeant Troy and felt that Fanny had thrown herself away. He then went on to show Oak Bathsheba's valentine. Her writing was identified. The valentine card brought confusion in the mind of Gabriel Oak and of Boldwood.

Glossary

followed at his heels	came soon after
she'll rue it	she'll regret it (that is, regret not having a bailiff)
conclave	meeting
epitome	a thing representing something else in miniature
keen weather	sharp, cold weather
aptitude	flair
condescension	air of superiority which makes one look down upon another
freak	unusual act
flushed	turn red as a result of strong emotion
qualm	an unpleasant feeling of being nervous or unsure

Comprehension

1. Summarise the conversation among the rustics. What impression do you get of them?
2. What brought Oak to the malthouse? How did he look after the newborn lambs?
3. What information did Fanny's letter communicate? What did it reveal about her and about Oak?
4. Describe in detail Boldwood's reaction to the news and his appraisal of Troy.
5. How does Boldwood react when he knows that Bathsheba had sent the valentine?
6. Assess Boldwood and Gabriel Oak as Bathsheba's suitors.

Chapter 15

Summary

A small crowd gathered at All Saints' Church in a remote barrack town. A smart young cavalry soldier in a red uniform walked up the aisle and stood at the altar railing. Obviously a wedding was about to take place and the crowd stayed on. The wait was long but there was no sign of the bride. The soldier eventually walked back in great embarrassment and went to the paved square opposite the church. There he met a little woman, presumably the bride, who looked anxious and afraid. She explained to the soldier that she had gone to All Souls' Church by mistake. She did not consider it a let-down and thought they could wed on the morrow, but Frank Troy who was utterly humiliated walked away.

Glossary

congregation	gathering
mouldy	old and decaying
nave	central part of the church building where the congregation sits
curate	a helper-priest of low rank
doffed his surplice	took off his robe
chancel	the part of the church near the altar, reserved for the clergy
titter	giggle
vestry	room or building attached to the church
expostulated	complained loudly

Comprehension

1. Describe the behaviour of the churchgoers. Why were they excited?
2. Give an account of Troy's entry into the church, his appearance, his expectation, his embarrassment and his exit.

3. How did Troy behave towards Fanny when he met her shortly afterwards?
4. What was Fanny's mistake? How did Troy react to her confession?
5. Do you think Troy's humiliation got the better of his love?
6. Is there any indication at the end of the chapter that Troy will marry Fanny?

CHAPTER 16

SUMMARY

Boldwood saw Bathsheba at the Casterbridge market-house and thought her beautiful. He was a rich farmer, tenant of Little Weatherbury Farm, with aristocratic leanings. He was a good-looking man who was inclined to seriousness in all his dealings. He was generally calm but was a man of strong and deep emotions. Bathsheba had not fully understood his nature when she played the practical joke on him. Boldwood came to the stable-door and looked across the meadow belonging to Bathsheba's farm. There he saw Bathsheba, Oak, and Cairny Ball. They were engaged in making an ewe (which had lost her offspring) 'take' to a substitute lamb. He decided to go over and speak to her. Bathsheba saw him and reddened visibly anticipating his visit. Boldwood moved on without entering her field. She was extremely troubled that she had played with Boldwood's emotions and resolved that she would never interfere in his life again. But the damage seemed already to have been done.

GLOSSARY

furtively	stealthily
credulous	ready to believe things
aristocracy	upper class
recessed	remote and secluded
obscure	not clear
equilibrium	balance

latent	hidden
ineradicable	something one cannot get rid of
exposure	act of being revealed
But a resolution to avoid an evil is seldom framed till the evil is so far advanced as to make avoidance impossible	a philosophic generalisation; human beings decide to avoid evil only when they are fully submerged in it and then it is usually too late.

Comprehension

1. Who is Boldwood's 'disturber' of 'dreams'? Why is she called so?
2. What features of Bathsheba's appearance did Boldwood single out as 'beautiful'?
3. Describe Boldwood's farm. What does it reveal about his station?
4. 'The phases of Boldwood's life were ordinary enough, but his was not an ordinary nature'. What does the statement imply? Comment in your own words Boldwood's appearance and temperament as presented in this chapter.
5. What was the task that engaged Gabriel and Bathsheba? Explain what you understand by it.
6. Boldwood had decided to meet Bathsheba. Why did he change his mind?
7. What was Bathsheba's resolve on seeing Boldwood? What does it say of her? Was she too late in arriving at her resolution?

Chapter 17

Summary

Three months after Valentine's Day at the end of May, Boldwood finally decided to call on Bathsheba. She was at the sheep washing pool watching her men performing the task with care and skill. She was dressed elegantly in a new riding habit. Boldwood found her more attractive than ever and greeted her. He made the offer of marriage which she received with a neutral countenance but with great agitation in her heart. She declined his offer and was profusely apologetic for her thoughtlessness concerning the valentine. Boldwood was serious in his mission and pressed on with his declarations of love. Bathsheba was deeply sympathetic and pleaded for time leaving Boldwood hopeful.

Glossary

flagon	a large container
cider	alcoholic drink made from apple juice
green	meadow
accentuated	emphasised
propriety	decency

Comprehension

1. Describe the sheep washing in your own words. What is Gabriel Oak's task?
2. How did Boldwood propose to Bathsheba? Comment on the words and phrases that reveal his passion?
3. What was Bathsheba's reaction? How was it conveyed?
4. What was the 'prophetic instinct' that Boldwood referred to?
5. Do you think Bathsheba was flirtatious or playful when she sent the valentine?
6. Describe Bathsheba's feelings. What is your impression of her?
7. What do you think of Boldwood in this situation?

Chapter 18

Summary

June was the sheep-shearing season and Bathsheba's men including Gabriel Oak were hard at work, some collecting the sheep, some shearing, and the women gathering the fleece.

Bathsheba was particularly attracted by Oak's speed and skill at his task. Boldwood appeared at this juncture and was greeted by Bathsheba. They talked quietly for a while before they rode away together. In the sight of the workers this implied a relationship which might end in matrimony. Oak was sad at this prospect but he still adored Bathsheba.

Glossary

culminated	ended
metamorphosed	transformed
bristle	stand on end
flitted	moved about
hovered	remained poised
lopped off	cut off
sleek	smooth
leanest pasture	the field where there was the scantiest growth of grass. Even this appeared green and fresh
Gold was palpably present in the country, and the devil had gone with the world to town	The appeal is to the imagination. The scene is one of peace and plenty.
'fixity of facial machinery'	the rooted or fixed expression on a person's face showing his concentration
'with a carriage of perfect ease'	in a manner free from embarrassment

Comprehension

1. Attempt a descriptive account of sheep shearing. What did Bathsheba admire about Oak's handiwork?
2. What transpired between Boldwood and Bathsheba in this chapter?
3. When they decided to ride out together, what do the rustics conclude?

4. What was Oak's reaction to what he sees?

CHAPTER 19

SUMMARY

Bathsheba sat at the head of the table for the shearing-supper. A happy Boldwood, cheerfully dressed and chatty, joined them. After supper Bathsheba occupied herself with knitting while Boldwood sat beside her. This was followed by a request from the workers that Bathsheba sing to them before they went home. Bathsheba sang charmingly and asked Gabriel to accompany her on the flute. The shearers left afterwards and Bathsheba and Boldwood were alone. He proposed to her again with sincerity and passion. Bathsheba, with tenderness and grace touched with firmness, asked him to wait.

GLOSSARY

eventide	evening
lustrously	with shine
blithe	happy, carefree
to an exceptional degree	to a very unusual degree
ochreous	yellowish
shearing-supper	sheep-shearing is an important event in the farm. When the shearing is over, the farmhands celebrate with a supper.
assented	agreed
coveted	much desired
tremulous	shaky
altar of applause	the best form of appreciation
sash	frame holding the glass in a window

Comprehension

1. Describe the arrangements for the shearing-supper. Where was Bathsheba seated?
2. For whom do you think was the seat at the bottom of the table left vacant?
3. Describe Boldwood's appearance and disposition.
4. Give an account of the entertainment that followed after the supper.
5. Describe the 'passionate scene' being enacted in the parlour.
6. Was there any progress made in the Boldwood–Bathsheba relationship? Comment.

Chapter 20

Summary

Bathsheba usually looked around the homestead to ensure that all was safe before going to bed. As she walked home through the fir plantation in the darkness that day, she heard the footsteps of a person entering the plantation at the opposite end. The dense foliage made the place seem dark even though it was only late in the evening. The man who entered the plantation glided past her when something tugged at her skirt which had got entangled in his spurs. He took a long time to free her. Finally she had to do it herself. He introduced himself as Sergeant Troy and spontaneously praised her for her beauty. When Bathsheba returned home, she gathered information from Liddy about Troy's antecedents. She too had been attracted to him and was happy with his compliments. She remembered that Boldwood never once praised her beauty.

Glossary

multifarious	varied
foliage	thick green leaves

'The contrast of this revelation . . . fairy transformation'	She expected a frightful creature, but saw a handsome soldier; it was like the happening in a fairy tale
spur	spiked device worn by a horse rider on the heel
gimp	a narrow piece of silk or cotton with a metallic wire running through it; used as trimming for dresses
obliquely	indirectly
chevrons	a piece of cloth in the shape . . . or V worn on the sleeve of an armed force soldier indicating rank
archness	coyness
sidled	walked away timidly
furlough	leave
'After all how could a cheerful wearer of skirts . . . told her she was beautiful'	The soldier complimented her beauty which pleased her. Boldwood had never done this.

Comprehension

1. What particular duty had Bathsheba assigned to herself since the departure of the bailiff?
2. As a storyteller, what techniques does Hardy use to make vivid the meeting of Troy and Bathsheba?
3. How does Troy speak to Bathsheba? What do you conclude about his behaviour and his nature? Use quotations to illustrate your answer.
4. Bathsheba had every reason to be annoyed with Troy but she was not. What do you think is the reason?
5. What did Liddy have to say about Troy?
6. What were Bathsheba's feelings after the incident at the plantation?
7. Why did Troy seem different from Boldwood, and more appealing?

CHAPTER 21

SUMMARY

Sergeant Troy was a man who lived in the present and was unconcerned about the past or the future and unruffled by moral values. He was always cheerful and easy-going which made him popular. On account of his education he talked pleasantly and appealingly. Truth was not very important to him and he lied especially to women. When he was not flattering women, he cursed them and swore at them. He didn't believe in treating them fairly. Bathsheba found Troy loading the hay on to the wagon along with her men. He greeted her, apologised profusely for his past behaviour and claimed he loved her. Bathsheba did not believe him but found herself greatly agitated by his attempts to please her.

GLOSSARY

idiosyncrasy	peculiarity
vicissitude	unpleasant circumstance
incumbrance /encumbrance	burden
superfluity	excess
cocks and windrows	hay is raked into long rows called windrows, then arranged in conical heaps called cocks
diminutive	extremely small
erratically flitting	skipping here and there unpredictably

COMPREHENSION

1. Describe Troy's traits that make him exceptional. What impression does the reader form of him?
2. From the description provided, what is the quality that stands out most? Which part of the description appeals to you?
3. How did Troy capitalise on his flaws?

4. What was Troy's attitude to women?
5. How was Bathsheba affected by her second meeting with Troy? How did she respond to his flirtatious behaviour?
6. How did Troy contrive to impress Bathsheba?
7. Examine the steps in the progress of the plot in this chapter.

CHAPTER 22

SUMMARY

As the farmhands were all busily engaged in saving the hay, Bathsheba decided to hive the bees herself. Taking all necessary precautions with gauze veil and gloves, she climbed the ladder. Just then Troy entered and asked her to let him assist her to do the job. She gave him her protective gear and he finished the task. Bathsheba then asked him about the sword exercises she had heard about and which he had casually mentioned. He promised to fetch his sword in the evening for a demonstration and whispered something to her. Bathsheba was agitated again, and with feigned reluctance agreed to go with him for a short while.

GLOSSARY

hiving the bees	the hive is dressed with honey and herbs to attract bees to settle in a man-made hive. As they swarm in and around the hive, they are brushed and helped in. The person carrying out this task uses gloves and a gauze veil.
impregnable	that which cannot be penetrated
flurry	troubled hurry
manoeuvre	a skilful move

Comprehension

1. Account for Troy's sudden appearance and Bathsheba's confusion.
2. What preparations were needed for the bee-hiving?
3. Hardy describes Troy's voice as having a 'strange power in agitating' Bathsheba. Why was this so?
4. Why do you think Troy offered to help Bathsheba with the bee-hiving task?
5. What was Bathsheba's innocent remark? What were the consequences?
6. Comment on the relationship between Troy and Bathsheba.

Chapter 23

Summary

Bathsheba agreed to meet Troy in the brake fern for the sword exercise that he would demonstrate using her as target. His was a splendid show of control and dexterity and Bathsheba came out of the dangerous performance unscathed. She had been adventurous and he had lied that his sharp sword was blunt. She was upset and Troy decided to retire with a lock of hair that he had cut. Before he left, he had kissed her and Bathsheba was overpowered by her feelings for Troy and her sense of sin from the encounter with him.

Glossary

'The bristling ball of gold in the west still swept the ferns with its rays when Bathsheba appeared in their midst, their soft feathery arms caressing her up to her shoulders.'	Note Hardy's poetic and vivid description. Even as the sun's golden rays fell on the fern, their soft leaves gently touched her.

brake fern	bracken; fern grown on waste land
temerity	boldness
relish	great satisfaction
flinch	move or shake
antagonist	opponent
infrequent light	brightness
broadsword	single-edged sword
fib	lie
brand	(poetic) sword
scabbard	the leather case worn at the belt in which the sword is housed

COMPREHENSION

1. Describe the landscape where Bathsheba met Troy. What words and phrases appeal to you in the description?
2. What were Bathsheba's feelings before the adventure?
3. How does Bathsheba participate in the sword exercise? What does Troy ask her to do? What is her query concerning the sword?
4. Pick out words, phrases which highlight Troy's skill. What is significant about the description?
5. What is Troy's comment about Bathsheba?
6. How did he cut the lock of hair? How did the meeting end?
7. What were Bathsheba's reactions? Why did Bathsheba feel guilty?
8. What do you think of the manner of Troy's departure?

SUMMARY

Gabriel had been troubled by Bathsheba's infatuation for Troy, and her unfair treatment of Boldwood. He met her when she was out for a short walk and confronted her with his anxieties. Bathsheba categorically stated her disinclination to marry Boldwood. Gabriel spoke of his distrust of Troy. Bathsheba reacted with annoyance and spoke of Troy as a god-fearing, church-going man. Gabriel spoke with sincerity and candour. He warned her concerning her dealings with the soldier and asked her to consider Boldwood's suit again – not even his. She was displeased with him for his interference. Gabriel left her, and soon after, found Bathsheba and Troy walking away. On his way home he discovered that the private entrance into the church had not been opened for a long time. Sergeant Troy had lied concerning his church attendance.

GLOSSARY

'Weakness is doubly weak by being new'	This is a generalisation of a trait. A strong person feels the impact of weakness more than a person who is already frail.
deformities	faults, weaknesses
embellishments	adornments
'whose defects were patent to the blindest and whose virtues were as metals in a mine.'	Troy and Oak as suitors of Bathsheba are compared. Troy's apparent attractive behaviour obscured his faults; Gabriel was straightforward and honest; his faults were visible and his virtues as yet undiscovered.
infatuation	strong unreasonable feeling of love
pensively	in deep reflection
unobscured	not hidden
spasmodic	irregular, not continuous
jamb	surface of a door

COMPREHENSION

1. How is Bathsheba's love for Troy contrasted with her respect for Boldwood?
2. Why is Gabriel Oak so concerned about Bathsheba? What reasons does he give to persuade her to leave Troy?

3. What is Bathsheba's stand with regard to Troy? Why is she annoyed with Oak?
4. What was it that Oak knew about Troy which made him wish that Bathsheba had never seen him?
5. Do you think that Oak should have revealed everything to Bathsheba?
6. What is the picture presented of Troy in this chapter? Contrast this with the characters of Boldwood and Oak.

CHAPTER 25

SUMMARY

Bathsheba was confused and perturbed by the sudden rush of love she felt for Troy. Troy had bid a brief farewell to her and had left for Bath to visit friends. Very impulsively, she wrote a letter to Boldwood saying that she had considered his proposal seriously but could not marry him. She went into the kitchen and was upset on hearing the gossip about her and Troy. She vehemently defended Troy and pleaded with Liddy to endorse her views. Love had become burdensome to Bathsheba. So had her beauty.

GLOSSARY

perturbed	upset
scamp	troublemaking person (a rather playful way of putting it)
surged	rushed
'Loving is misery for women always'	According to Bathsheba, to be in love is great suffering for a woman—is it due to the lover who is not good enough or is it because there are many suitors who court a beautiful woman?

Comprehension

1. Why is this chapter called 'Hot cheeks and Tearful eyes' Illustrate with specific examples.
2. What made Bathsheba write the letter to Boldwood?
3. How did she see her relationship with Troy? How do you see it?
4. Why was she angry when her maids condemned Troy?
5. What was her confession to Liddy?
6. Why do you think Bathsheba is so emotionally disturbed regarding her relationship?

Chapter 26

Summary

Bathsheba anticipated Boldwood's visit on seeing her letter. In order to avoid him she set out for Liddy's the evening of the following day. However on the way Boldwood appeared. He passionately expressed his love for her; he said he loved her intensely and he believed her refusal to marry him was a jest (even as the valentine was). Bathsheba tried to convince him that it was not so. Boldwood then revealed that her refusal of him was on account of Troy who now had a claim on her affections. Boldwood had probably seen them together. He vowed revenge on Troy. Bathsheba was in a dilemma and decided to rush to Bath that night to see Troy.

Glossary

getting out of the way	avoiding
supplicate	to beg earnestly and humbly
a stone's throw	very near
groove	channel
stoic	a person who shows no feelings of like or dislike when faced with unpleasantness
untimely stripling	young man (contemptuous reference)

inert	lacking strength and vigour
shrew	bad-tempered, scolding woman
denunciations	public condemnation
gratuitous	uncalled for
'Boldwood's ideas had reached that point of fusion at which outline and consistency entirely disappear.'	Boldwood was so deeply hurt by Bathsheba's disclosure of love of Troy that he was incoherent and angry.

Comprehension

1. How and why did Bathsheba try to avoid Boldwood? Did she succeed in doing so?
2. Describe Boldwood's changed appearance and manner.
3. What arguments did Boldwood put forward to convince Bathsheba that she should accept him?
4. What was Bathsheba's reply? What do you think of her reaction and behaviour in this situation?
5. How did Boldwood know that Troy was his rival? How did he behave thereafter?
6. Describe in detail Bathsheba's feelings and analyse her decision.
7. Why is this chapter important in furthering the plot?

Chapter 27

Summary

A note sent to Maryann indicated that Bathsheba would be away on business in Bath. Two weeks had passed. One day during the oat-harvest, Cain Ball dressed in his best accosted the farm workers. He was on holiday due to a sore finger and had gone away to Bath. There he had seen Bathsheba with a soldier who he thought was Sergeant Troy. He had seen them behave like courting couples, he said. Oak was greatly disturbed by the news and wanted him to swear by God at which Cain Ball hesitated. But Oak knew the truth and felt downcast.

GLOSSARY

harbinger	person or thing that announces the approach of something or someone
whetting	sharpening the blade
scythe	tool with curved blade for cutting crops
sojer	soldier
in the most awful form	a strong oath like 'I swear to God'
a'most	almost
mane	mean
felon	a sore finger, whitlow
a said	he said
hollerday	holiday
I've seed	I've seen
byemeby	by and by
arm-in-crook	arm-in-arm

COMPREHENSION

1. What were the contents of the note to Maryann?
2. Who was the figure in the 'blue coat and brass buttons'? Describe him and his state of mind.
3. What made the workers suspend their work?
4. Give a detailed account of Cain Ball's experience in Bath.
5. What was Oak's reaction?
6. How did Oak try to get at the truth?
7. What was Coggan's counsel?
8. Comment on Hardy's technique of continuing the story through a minor character. What effect does it create?

CHAPTER 28

SUMMARY

Gabriel was very relieved to see that Bathsheba and Liddy had returned safely the same evening. Boldwood went to Bathsheba's house to apologise for his earlier behaviour but she refused to meet with him. On the way back he met Troy. Boldwood put it to him authoritatively that he should leave Bathsheba alone and marry Fanny Robin instead and was prepared to give him some money to quit Weatherbury. Troy agreed, but asked Boldwood to listen in on a conversation between him and Bathsheba as they would be meeting shortly. Boldwood did, and was shocked to hear Bathsheba's endearments towards Troy and her invitation to him to spend the night at her house. Convinced that Bathsheba was throwing herself away misguidedly, Boldwood entreated Troy to marry her, and said that he would give her up. Then Troy showed him the news item from the papers which carried their wedding announcement. Boldwood was dazed with all this revelation and in his agitation paced the length and breadth of Weatherbury that night.

Glossary

gig	horse-driven carriage
cudgel	thick stick
civil	polite
stalwart frame	well-built, muscular body
deluded woman	a woman who has been deceived
downs	valleys (common in the countryside of England)

Comprehension

1. What was Bathsheba's reason for the long absence from home?
2. Why was Gabriel relieved to see her return?
3. What was Boldwood's reason for visiting Bathsheba? What does this say of Boldwood?
4. What was Boldwood's attitude towards Troy on meeting him? What did he propose to him?
5. Why did Boldwood later ask Troy to marry Bathsheba?
6. Comment on Troy's behaviour in this chapter. What does it show of his character?

7. Does the news of Bathsheba's marriage come as a surprise to us as it does to Boldwood? Is Troy a trickster?
8. Comment on Hardy's handling of the way in which Bathsheba is divested of two of her suitors.

Chapter 29

Summary

When Coggan and Oak arrived at the field early the next morning, they saw from a distance, Troy at an upper window in their mistress's house. Gabriel was upset on realising that Troy had married Bathsheba. As they approached the house, Troy greeted them and told them he wanted to modernise the house. He gave them a half-crown to drink to his health much to Gabriel's annoyance. As they left, Coggan advised Gabriel to seem friendly to Troy who might be their future master. A horseman approached and passed by them. It was a visibly suffering Mr Boldwood.

Glossary

lattice	window pane made up of diagonal strips of lead
listlessly	lacking enthusiasm
a time of sun and dew	a picturesque and poetic expression for dawn
candour	openness; frankness
buy his discharge	A soldier is allowed to leave the army on paying a certain amount of money
troublehouse	troublemaker, source of trouble

Comprehension

1. Who was the man who looked out of the window? What was he doing?

2. What was Coggan's remark on seeing him? How did Gabriel react?
3. What was Troy's attitude in accosting them?
4. What did Troy mean when he said, 'I feel like new wine in an old bottle'?
5. What did it reveal about his nature?
6. What does Coggan's advice imply: 'Therefore 'tis well to say "Friend" outwardly, though you say "Troublehouse" within'?
7. Describe Boldwood's appearance and his state of mind. How did Gabriel react to Boldwood?

Chapter 30

Summary

Sergeant Troy hosted a harvest supper and dance on a night in August when thunder and rain were imminent. Oak was concerned that the ricks had to be protected and he tried to warn Troy. Troy ignored the advice, and having dismissed the women from the scene, wanted to celebrate the harvest and his wedding by serving brandy. Bathsheba left in anger. Oak also took his leave. On his way he realised that there would be rain and turned back to cover the ricks. He resolved to save the harvested crops for the sake of Bathsheba, the woman he loved. He returned to the barn for assistance and found Troy asleep and the farmhands drunk; Oak worked alone.

Glossary

wealth in jeopardy	wealth in danger
revel	noisy party
appropriated	taken for use
rostrum	raised platform
juxtaposition	side by side
stepped ath'art	stepped athwart or across
such fidgets	such worries
carouse	lively party with drinks
the Great Mother	Nature
deteriorating	becoming worse

Comprehension

1. What were the signs in nature that Gabriel read as foretelling a storm?
2. Describe the harvest supper celebrations and Troy's personal contribution to it.
3. What was Troy's response when he was warned of the impending storm?
4. Why did Bathsheba leave the barn? What happened to Troy and the farmhands afterwards?
5. Why do you think the party becomes insignificant in the face of the storm?
6. What action did Oak take to protect the grain from the storm?
7. Why did Oak take it upon himself to save the harvest? Why was he alone? Note the proximity of nature to rural folk and life on the farm.

Chapter 31

Summary

The storm broke when Gabriel was at work. Bathsheba came out and helped him. She was truly grateful to him for his timely help and devotion. It was a terrible storm – the loud thunder, the flash of lightning and the downpour. They worked together and soon the storm abated. Bathsheba used this opportunity to explain under what circumstances she had married Troy, and the nature of her tumultuous feelings. . She thanked Gabriel for his devotion and left on his persuasion.

Glossary

A light flapped ..... Rumbles became rattles	Hardy presents a vivid and visual description of the storm.
flare	burning with a bright flame
diabolical	evil and unpleasant

aerial perch	referring to the ladder
broached	raised, introduced
impetuosity	hasty action
reverie	dream
infuriated	angered

Comprehension

1. Pick out the descriptive phrases picturing the storm. Attempt your own version of the awe-inspiring scene.
2. What was the effect of the storm on Gabriel and Bathsheba?
3. Recount Bathsheba's explanation to Gabriel concerning her marriage to Troy.
4. 'And then, between jealousy and distraction I married him!' What does this say of Bathsheba?
5. How did Gabriel console her and show that he understood her predicament?
6. What aspects of the character of Gabriel and Bathsheba are revealed in this chapter?

Chapter 32

Summary

Bathsheba and Troy (now a farmer) were returning from the market. Bathsheba was despondent and angry because her husband had squandered her money on horse-racing. She feared that the farm would be lost if this reckless spending continued. Troy made fun of her for being faint-hearted. On the way, a shabbily dressed woman accosted them asking the way to Casterbridge Union House. On recognising her as Fanny, Troy followed her and fixed an appointment to help her. Bathsheba queried Troy concerning the woman. He answered her evasively.

Glossary

Casterbridge Union House	In England, there used to be union houses (poor houses or work houses) where poor people who had no place to stay were housed.

Comprehension

1. 'Bathsheba, you have lost all the pluck and sauciness you formerly had.' Why did Troy make such a statement? Was it a justifiable statement?
2. Do you think Bathsheba is responsible for the state she is in? Discuss.
3. Comment on the relationship between Troy and Bathsheba before and after marriage.
4. What do you think was Troy's motive in marrying Bathsheba?
5. Who was the poor woman they met on the road? How did she and Troy respond to each other?
6. Where was she going? What was Troy's message to her?
7. What was Bathsheba's reaction?
8. Describe the woman's condition.

Chapter 33

Summary

Troy asked Bathsheba that evening to give him twenty pounds. When he realised she was suspicious of him, he protested against her attitude. She gave him the money. Before he left he opened his watch case and she caught sight of the curl of yellow hair that had been preserved in it. Troy told her it belonged to the woman he had loved before he met Bathsheba. Bathsheba was greatly distressed. Her pride was hurt. The following morning Troy rose early and left for Casterbridge. Bathsheba took a walk and came to know from Joseph Poorgrass that Fanny Robin had died in the Union House in Casterbridge, and that Boldwood was making arrangements for the funeral. Bathsheba was shocked on hearing the news. It dawned on her, on further investigation, that the woman who had passed them on the turnpike road the previous evening had been Fanny Robin. She felt duty bound to send for Fanny's corpse as she had been an employee on her farm. She sent Joseph Poorgrass with her wagon to bring the corpse to her farmhouse.

Glossary

strait-waistcoating	such restriction and lecturing
got handy the Union-house	reached the Union House
traipsed	walked
fainty	as if about to faint

Comprehension

1. Why did Troy require twenty pounds? What was Bathsheba's suspicion?
2. What does Troy accuse Bathsheba of?
3. What was Troy's explanation about the lock of hair?
4. 'O, if she had never stooped to folly of this kind'. What does this refer to, and what does it imply?
5. What information did Joseph Poorgrass pass on to Bathsheba? How did she react?
6. What do you think of Boldwood's actions with regard to Fanny?
7. What did Bathsheba discover about Fanny?

CHAPTER 34

SUMMARY

At three in the afternoon, Joseph Poorgrass arrived at the workhouse to take away Fanny's coffin. A rough inscription was written on it in chalk. Poorgrass placed the flowers he had brought on the coffin and placed it in the wagon. The formalities being over, he set out for Weatherbury. At the sight of the Buck's Head Inn, Poorgrass could not resist the urge to have a drink. He met his drinking companions, Jan Coggan and Mark Clark there and spent the evening drinking, oblivious of his burdensome assignment. Gabriel Oak arrived there and seeing Poorgrass in a drunken state took charge of the operation. The parson met him on his getting to the manor-house but felt it was too late in the evening for the funeral to be held. So Gabriel decided to take the coffin to Bathsheba's house for the night. She insisted on taking it inside. Before leaving, Gabriel rubbed out 'and child' from the inscription 'Fanny Robin and child', to save Bathsheba immediate anguish.

GLOSSARY

enjoined	requested
contingencies	emergencies
repeater	a watch with a striking mechanism

COMPREHENSION

1. How did Poorgrass take charge of the coffin at the Casterbridge Union-house?
2. What did Poorgrass do on reaching Buck's Head Inn?
3. Why did he say his journey was not pleasant?
4. Why did the parson refuse to hold the funeral that evening?
5. What did Gabriel decide to do?
6. 'It is unkind and unchristian,' said Bathsheba. What did this refer to? What did she mean?

7. What was the final act of kindness on Gabriel's part before his departure?
8. Comment on Gabriel's role in this chapter, and Bathsheba's response to the sequence of events.

Chapter 35

Summary

Alone and miserable, Bathsheba waited for her husband's return home while Fanny lay in the coffin in the room next to the hall. Liddy informed Bathsheba of the rumour she had heard that Fanny had had a child. Bathsheba was shocked and intensely grief-stricken. Her curiosity overcame her and she opened the coffin to verify the truth of the report. Her worst fears were confirmed. Her husband came in and seeing Fanny's corpse was shocked and stricken with remorse. He kissed the dead woman and called her his wife. His posturing filled Bathsheba with pain and anguish. When she provoked him for a response he said Bathsheba meant nothing to him and that their marriage was a marriage in name only. Bathsheba fled from the scene.

Glossary

'Bathsheba was lonely and miserable now . . . a mountain is to the solitude of a cave.'	Loneliness is an aspect of life irrespective of individual status. Bathsheba's loneliness after marriage was more intense and confining than before. Hardy uses 'nature' similes to describe it.
solicitousness	eager or anxious to do something
lurid sheen	unnaturally bright shine

Comprehension

1. Why was Bathsheba so lonely and miserable?
2. What did Liddy reveal as 'strange news'?
3. What were Bathsheba's feelings on hearing the news? Why did she decide to open the coffin?
4. Describe Bathsheba's condition after she opened the coffin.
5. What was Troy's reaction when he entered and saw the coffin?
6. 'I have been a bad, black-hearted man.' What does Troy imply by this statement?
7. 'If she's that, what am I?' What prompted this remark, and what is its significance?
8. What is Troy's reply? What does this reveal of his character?
9. Comment on the title of this chapter, 'Fanny's Revenge.'

Chapter 36

Summary

Troy waited miserably for the morning. He cast his mind back over the past twenty four hours. Fanny had failed to keep her appointment with him on Grey's Bridge on Monday morning—she was already dead. He had made no enquiries though but assumed she had failed him a second time. In anger he had gone off to the races and come home to the fearful shock that awaited him. As soon as it was morning, Troy took all the money he had and approached a marble mason to make a good tombstone. He returned in the afternoon to collect it and erect it in the Weatherbury churchyard. Bathsheba visited the churchyard and saw the grand tomb erected by Francis Troy for Fanny Robin.

Glossary

stalked	went cautiously
churchyard	a cemetery within the church premises
crocketed	carved

Comprehension

1. Troy took money from Bathsheba to help Fanny. Why did he fail to meet her?
2. What happened to Fanny at the poorhouse?
3. After his return home, what did Troy do?
4. Do you think erecting a marble tombstone could make amends for the wrongs done to Fanny?
5. What do you infer about Troy and his dealings with women?
6. Why did Bathsheba visit Fanny's grave? What did she see there?
7. Comment on the irony in the title of this chapter, 'Troy's Romanticism.'

Chapter 37

Summary

With mixed feelings of grief, remorse and hatred, Troy left Weatherbury. He decided to take a swim in the sea and was carried away by an unexpected tide. A ship's boat with many sailors came his way and he was rescued.

Glossary

a composite feeling	different feelings put together
indelible	that cannot be forgotten
averseness	hatred
ocean swell	referring to the waves
hauled	pulled up
roadstead	a protected place where ships can anchor

Comprehension

1. Describe Troy's state of mind when he left Weatherbury.
2. What happened to Troy when he was in the sea?

3. How did Troy save himself? How did the ship's crew take care of him?

Chapter 38

Summary

Bathsheba reacted to her husband's absence with mixed feelings—surprise, relief, and even indifference. On her visit to Casterbridge she passed the market-house where the businessmen from the countryside had gathered. There she encountered a man who said he was looking for her. He brought the news that her husband had drowned. She fainted immediately and Boldwood, who had been watching her, offered to take her home in his carriage. She refused and drove home herself. She told Liddy that she had the conviction Troy was still alive. However the newspaper report spoke of an eye-witness to the accident that Troy was involved in at sea. Troy's clothes were also eventually returned to her.

Glossary

invigorated	energised
flushed	became red and hot
phaeton	a light four-wheeled open carriage drawn by two horses
fuze	fuse

Comprehension

1. What were Bathsheba's feelings when her husband did not return for several days?
2. On her visit to Casterbridge, what news did the stranger give Bathsheba?
3. What was Bathsheba's reaction to the news?

4. What made her say 'It is not true!' and later to Liddy, 'I am perfectly convinced that he is alive.'?
5. Comment on Boldwood's reaction and his offer to take her home.
6. What do you think of Bathsheba in this chapter?
7. What does the 'fuze to this great explosion' mean and imply?
8. Why did Bathsheba decide not to destroy Fanny's lock of hair?
9. The title of this chapter reads, 'Doubts arise – Doubts linger'. Summarise the doubts that 'arise' and those that 'linger' in relation to the unfolding events.

Chapter 39

Summary

Time elapsed since Troy's disappearance. The sheep fair was being held at Weatherbury. It was a merry, noisy and busy gathering on a level green space of ten acres or so on the top of a hill. Gabriel as Bathsheba's bailiff, and Boldwood's shepherd, was there and looked after their flocks. In another part of the hill there was a circus tent and Sergeant Troy was seen sitting there, putting on his jack-boots. Troy had become a performer in the travelling circus. He had made his way to the United States where he worked as Professor of Gymnastics and Fencing. On his return to England he had joined the travelling circus. Bathsheba sat as a 'reserved' spectator at the show. Troy was to play the part of Turpin. On seeing Bathsheba at the circus, he was afraid of being recognised and exposed. He later decided to befriend Pennyways, Bathsheba's former bailiff, whom he met at the circus.

Glossary

precarious	dangerous
concurrence	agreement
brig	American name for a ship

Comprehension

1. Describe the sheep fair. What was Oak's responsibility?
2. What happened to Troy after his 'supposed' drowning? How did he make a living?
3. Why did he return to England?
4. Describe Troy's part in the circus-show. What were his feelings on seeing Bathsheba who was a spectator?
5. What did Troy do to avoid being detected by his wife?
6. Who recognised Troy? What was Troy's plan in seeking his friendship?
7. Comment on how Hardy describes the fair and the circus show.
8. How would you describe Troy's return and his role in this chapter?

Summary

Oak should have driven Bathsheba home to Weatherbury, but Boldwood, whom she met by chance at the refreshment-tent, offered to be her escort on horseback. Bathsheba agreed, convinced never to treat Boldwood unfairly again. Boldwood broached the subject of marriage and asked if Bathsheba would marry again some day. Even though there was no absolute certainty that Troy was dead, an interval of six years would give Bathsheba the freedom to marry again. Boldwood recollected the past and entreated her to 'make amends' by giving her consent to marry him after six years had elapsed. Bathsheba was in a state of confusion seeing how persistent and excited Boldwood was. She asked him to wait till Christmas for an answer.

Glossary

outrider	guard or attendant riding by the side
wending ways	moving slowly
point-blank query	direct question, without mincing words
elapsed	went by, passed by

Comprehension

1. Why do you think Boldwood wanted to escort Bathsheba? What made her consent to this?
2. Why did Boldwood talk of marriage? What arguments did he put forward to persuade Bathsheba into marrying him?
3. How did Bathsheba respond to these arguments? What are Bathsheba's feelings towards Boldwood?
4. Comment on the Boldwood–Bathsheba relationship.

Chapter 41

Summary

It was Christmas Eve and Boldwood was to give a party—he had not attempted this before. Preparations were on in full swing. Bathsheba, for whom the party was being given, dressed reluctantly to go to it. Boldwood took great care to dress for the occasion. There was a feverish anxiety and excitement in his manner. Troy was at Casterbridge in the company of the dishonest Pennyways. He was curious to know if there were legal implications in his 'return from the dead'. He had left the travelling circus and was preparing to go and meet Bathsheba. She was wealthy and secure with a house and farm while he was a poor and needy adventurer. He was also anxious to know her mind, and find out the truth about her relationship with Boldwood.

Glossary

converging courses	paths or ways of action that come to meet
incongruous	not appropriate
sits upon me	fits me/ suits me
fastidious	difficult to please, fussy
wadn'	was not

Comprehension

1. Why was a party at Boldwood's described in the chapter as 'abnormal' and 'incongruous'?
2. What was a. Bathsheba's state of mind, b. Boldwood's state of mind? Compare and contrast their situations.
3. 'I have never been free from trouble since I have lived here and this party is likely to bring more.' What are the implications of Bathsheba's statement?
4. Why did Troy want to return to Bathsheba? Comment.
5. Why did Troy disguise himself?
6. Are there premonitions of tragedy in this chapter? Illustrate.

Chapter 42

Summary

Outside Boldwood's house, the men were talking in whispers and decided to speak to their master regarding the stranger there. As the party got underway, Bathsheba felt she had stayed long enough and prepared to leave. Boldwood raised the issue of marriage again and made her promise to marry him after six years—the time to decide that Troy would never return. Bathsheba was quite distressed but she gave him her word. When she came downstairs she was approached by a man who told her a stranger wished to speak with her. Bathsheba recognised the stranger as Troy. He asked her to accompany him. Boldwood realised what was happening. Troy tried to force Bathsheba. She screamed. A shot was heard. Boldwood had shot Troy. He then tried to shoot himself but was prevented. He kissed Bathsheba's hand and went out into the darkness.

Glossary

'Concurritur– Horae Momento'	The title is part of a quotation from Horace's *Satires*. Translated, it reads as 'battle is joined, and in a moment

	of time comes speedy death or joyous recovery.'
'baint	are not
evasion	avoidance of the issue
give up	to surrender
askance	with distrust

Comprehension

1. Give an account of the discussion outside Boldwood's house.
2. Who was the stranger? Why did he disguise himself?
3. 'If he is alive and here in the neighbourhood, he means mischief'. What does this refer to? How is it related to the action in this chapter?
4. How did Boldwood persuade Bathsheba to agree to marry him after six years?
5. How did she respond?
6. What did Troy tell Bathsheba on meeting her? What was her reaction?
7. How did Boldwood react? Make a studied analysis of his feelings.
8. Why did Boldwood shoot Troy? Was it a premeditated act?
9. Is this the climax of the story? Discuss.

Chapter 43

Summary

Boldwood left his house and went to Casterbridge and surrendered at the prison. Gabriel Oak heard of the shooting and went to Boldwood's house. There, Bathsheba was on the floor, distraught, with Troy's head on her lap. She appealed to Oak to bring the doctor though it seemed useless. When Oak arrived with the doctor he found that Bathsheba had left for her house. Oak reached the place and found that Bathsheba had stoically prepared and laid out Troy's body for the funeral. She was exhausted and had to be given medical aid.

GLOSSARY

gaol	another (older) way of spelling jail
coma	state of unconsciousness
traversed	travelled across
stoic	a person who is indifferent to pain
fortitude	courage in bearing suffering

COMPREHENSION

1. How did Boldwood leave home and give himself up? What does it say of Boldwood?
2. How did Bathsheba react to the shock of Troy's death? What did she do?
3. 'She was of the stuff of which great men's mothers are made.' Explain.
4. 'The heart of a wife merely'. Explain this phrase and comment on Bathsheba's character.

CHAPTER 44

SUMMARY

Bathsheba had suspected for some time that Boldwood was mentally deranged. This was attested by the discovery in his locked closet of an extraordinary collection of articles—dresses to suit Bathsheba, sable and ermine muffs, and jewellery, all marked 'Bathsheba Boldwood' and dated six years in advance. All this indicated a mind crazed with love. Boldwood had pleaded guilty to his crime and was sentenced to death. However, through a petition to the Home Secretary from the people of Weatherbury, this was changed to life imprisonment.

Glossary

mental derangement	disorder of the mind
muffs	made of fur, worn over the hands to keep warm
sable and ermine	kinds of animal fur
upshot	the end result
solicitous	showing concern

Comprehension

1. What is the evidence of Boldwood's mental derangement? Can you find examples of this in the earlier chapters?
2. What do the people of Weatherbury think of Boldwood?
3. Describe Bathsheba's feelings. What were Oak's feelings towards Boldwood?
4. What was the sentence on Boldwood? How was it changed?
5. What is the effect of this change on the people of Weatherbury?

Chapter 45

Summary

As time passed, Bathsheba recovered and resumed her routine farming activities. She walked to see the grave of Fanny Robin. She was upset on seeing the tombstones of Fanny and Troy. The inscription on Troy's tombstone had been done according to her instructions. Oak met her in the churchyard and walking back with her told her of his plans to leave Weatherbury. Bathsheba was visibly upset. That evening she decided to visit Oak. He told her he would not emigrate and made her aware of the gossip that surrounded them. When asked if she would marry him she immediately assented. Their love which had its basis in friendship had withstood the test of time.

Glossary

'Bathsheba revived with the spring'	Bathsheba regained her health
shunned	avoided, ignored
sombre	serious
preternatural	beyond what is normal or natural
Lady-day	25 March; a feast of the Virgin Mary, the day on which engagements usually lapsed
the top and tail of it	the gist of it
interstices	intervening spaces
camaraderie	mutual trust and friendship
evanescent	short-lived

Comprehension

1. What were Bathsheba's thoughts and feelings at the beginning of the chapter?
2. What is significant about Fanny's and Troy's tombstones?
3. Account for Bathsheba's sadness and helplessness after Oak spoke to her.
4. Why did Oak want to leave Weatherbury? What did he plan to do?
5. Why did Bathsheba visit Oak? Relate what transpired between them.
6. What did they decide to do finally?
7. How is the friendship/relationship between Bathsheba and Gabriel Oak described?
8. Comment on the ending of the novel.

CRITICAL ESSAYS

1. *'Far from the Madding Crowd*

George Harvey

Far from the Madding Crowd is strongly influenced by the world of the ballad, but as its title—a line from Gray's 'Elegy Written in a Country Churchyard'—suggests, it also celebrates the removed rural life. Hardy described *Far from the Madding Crowd* [21–2]* as a pastoral tale (LW, 98). He underlined this by allusions to Milton's *Lycidas* and Virgil's *Georgics,* and by having in his hero Gabriel Oak, a shepherd who could play his flute with 'Arcadian sweetness' (*FFMC,* 6). This romantic, patient lover of Bathsheba Everdene is the chief representative of Hardy's pastoral ideal, a 'pastoral king' (*FFMC,* 6) as he calls him, whose 'Pastoral Tragedy' (*FFMC,* 5) the loss of his sheep, has reduced his status to that of a hired man on Bathsheba's farm. Oak retains a quiet authority partly through his associations with the values of an idyllic pastoral world. He naturally courts Bathsheba by taking her a present of an orphaned lamb. However, the elements of pastoral are rooted with compelling realism in the rituals of the farming calendar, such as sheep shearing and harvesting, and in the social events that structure and give meaning to the life of the agricultural community. Hardy gives a voice to the community through the workfolk who meet at Warren's Malthouse: Poorgrass, Coggan, Tall, Fray and others. They are presented without condescension, speaking in authentic dialect, and they are a source of gossip and humour. As a repository of traditional rural wisdom, they also provide a sense of living culture, against which the main characters are judged.

The symbolic centre and spiritual heart of *Far from the Madding Crowd* is the Great Barn, a grand medieval structure in which the sheep-shearing taking place. Hardy is at pains to emphasise the harmony between the shearers and the barn, and the continued relevance of the building to the life of the community. Unlike the

All parenthetical references to the text are from the original edition of *Far from the Madding Crowd,* and not the present one.

other medieval buildings, the church and the castle, 'the old barn embodied practices which had suffered no mutilation at the hands of time' (*FFMC*, 22). By extension, as Hardy suggests the sheep shearing. 'This picture of to-day in its frame of four hundred years ago' stands for the village of Weatherbury, which in comparison with cities was 'immutable' (*FFMC*, 22).

The even-tenored life of the rural community is distributed by the arrival of a woman farmer in Bathsheba, who has inherited her uncle's term, and who is placed in a traditionally masculine role. This is challenged by the dramatic appearance of Frank Troy, a figure from the world of ballad, a dashing sergeant of cavalry, of good family and education, who is also a mercurial, sexually predatory scapegrace. Troy's sexual awakening of Bathsheba is achieved in the famous scene of his sword drill (which Hardy researched), with its erotic symbolism of penetration, in 'the hollow amid the ferns' (*FFMC*, 28), as he fascinates and dominates her, enforcing his sexual mastery. His rootless modernity is also a disruptive element in Weatherbury. He has no feeling of responsibility to the farming community. Stupefied by drink after the harvest supper, he is oblivious to the vulnerability of the ricks to the coming storm. He also lacks the countryman's sense of continuity and time (symbolically he offers his watch to Bathsheba), and has no feeling either for the rhythms of nature. One of Troy's functions in the narrative is to upset the ordered pattern of rural life.

Hardy gave no hint to Leslie Stephen, in his original suggestion for the novel, that Bathsheba would occupy its central role. It is evident that Hardy was interested in the complexity of her psychology, particularly in relation to her own sense of identity. An intelligent, capable woman, she almost ruins her life by her sexual responses to the men who pursue her. She seems to fear the moral power bestowed on Oak by virtue of his critical observation of her; she is almost beaten down by the social expectation of marriage following Farmer Boldwood's receipt of her Valentine; but she feels sinful in the sexual abandon of her surrender to Troy. Yet in this relationship she succumbs to her fundamental desire to have her independent spirit tamed in a way that she knows Oak could never do.

The narrative seeks to emphasise the conflictual condition of her mind. Initially, she is presented from the point of view of Gabriel Oak, who is observing her as she sits on a wagon, narcissistically regarding her own extraordinary beauty in a small looking glass, conjecturally dreaming of triumphs over men. She uses her sexuality as a form of defence and control. Hardy describes her as a woman whose independence of men is necessary to her sense of identity, and who regards marriage as literally a degrading sacrifice of self. Her experience with Sergeant Troy is profoundly de-stabilising, when she finally realizes how her selfhood is bound with her passion for him at the moment he kisses the dead Fanny Robin, his wife, as he says in the sight of heaven because of their previous sexual relationship. After the shooting of Troy, the proud Bathsheba is brought to utter prostration. The complexity of Bathsheba's presentation is a source of critical debate, particularly among feminist critics of the novel (185, 186, 188).

Hardy uses the social ritual of the Valentine to complex effect. It symbolizes that combination of character, accident, and social convention that characterizes the operation of the world of Hardy's novels. For Bathsheba, sending the Valentine is a whimsical freak, originating with Liddy. The working of chance is symbolized by the tossing of a hymn book to decide whether the recipent is to be little Teddy Coggan or William Boldwood. Boldwood is transfixed by it, 'till the large red seal became as a blot of blood on the retina of his eye' (*FFMC*, 14). This imagery is proleptic of sex and death. The solitude of his home has been penetrated, and the regular pattern of his life is about to be tragically disrupted by an overwhelming obsession.

Evidence from the manuscript of the novel suggests that William Boldwood was introduced at a later stage of composition. His entry into the text provided Hardy with a powerful contrast between Troy's instinctive understanding of women and Boldwood's sexual obtuseness. Boldwood is a penetrating study of an obsessive personality, whose sexual desires, sublimated in the successful running of Little Weatherbury Farm, once awakened dominate him. Boldwood's courtship, subtly understood by Gabriel Oak, although superficially social and doggedly persistent, is also pathologically sexual. His life subsequently adopts the pattern of tragic drama.

His pursuit of Bathsheba is thwarted, on the point of her yielding to the sheer pressure of his presence, by the sudden arrival of Frank Troy. Boldwood's ignominious public collapse on the occasion of Bathsheba's marriage to Troy has serious social consequences when he fails to secure his ricks against the great storm. Baffled again by Troy's reappearance to claim his wife at the Christmas party at which Boldwood has just coerced her into a promise of their future engagement, he acknowledges Troy's authority over his wife, but her cry when she is touched by him releases the rage that prompts him to shoot the soldier dead.

The full tragic implication of this act Hardy reserves for the discovery in a locked closet in Boldwood's home of expensive lady's dresses, and a case of jewelry, accumulated secretly, labelled 'Bathsheba Boldwood', each dated six years in advance. This fetishism and obsessive ferocity for possession produces sympathy for Boldwood and makes acceptable his reprieve from the gallows after his failed suicide attempt. However, he is thwarted yet again in his surrender to the police and his desire for the oblivion of death, and he is forced to live out his obsession to the end.

The melodramatic climax to the narrative of the two rivals clears the way for Gabriel Oak, who has channelled his love into devotion and service, and who earns his reward through trials of his merit. The eventual union of Oak and Bathsheba is foreshadowed from the beginning by her evident disturbance at his proposal of marriage in a scene that carries a strong undercurrent of sexual tension. Also proleptic is the intensely visual, symbolic scene in which Gabriel and Bathsheba work together to thatch the rick – the harvest on which the community depends – before the rain comes, silhouetted by lightning – in which each acknowledges the other's true worth.

The novel's closing scenes inversely parallel Gabriel's early courtship. Again Bathsheba pursues him but this time prompts him to renew his offer. Both have matured through experience Gabriel Oak represents the stoical endurance of a man who has learnt to work with the unpredictability of nature, the volatility of women, and to discipline his own feelings and conduct. Bathsheba represents the achievement of a true sense of self-worth, and the clear-sighted recognition of human values. Now that Oak is taking the tenure of Boldwood's farm they are social equals, who between them will maintain the village community.

Low-key domestic realism at the conclusion supports the symbolism of the continuity of rural values and a profounder love deepened by friendship that supplants mere passion. They walk to their wedding on a damp and misty morning.

The narrative of *Far from the Madding Crowd* is designed to suit publication in serial form. As well as the contrast established between Bathsheba's three suitors, there is a deliberate contrast between the fate of Bathsheba and that of Fanny Robin. They are linked through Fanny's meeting Gabriel Oak on the road to Warren's Malthouse, through Fanny's employment by Bathsheba, and through her relationship with Troy. The traditional ballad tale of the young rural servant girl seduced and betrayed by a soldier tactfully counterpoints the main story. The height of Bathsheba's success as a new woman farmer – introducing herself with authority as the mistress of Weatherbury Upper Farm, and entering the male world of the Casterbridge corn market – frame Fanny Robin's pleading in the snow outside Troy's barracks from across the river. Bathsheba's marriage to Troy at Bath is matched by Fanny's death in the Union of Casterbridge. Her death also signals the death of Bathsheba's marriage. Although the chapter in which Bathsheba discovers the baby in Fanny's coffin is entitled 'Fanny's Revenge', Hardy avoids melodrama. It is an emotionally powerful scene in which both Troy and Bathsheba are forced to be true to their own natures in confronting the past. It is a richly visual, deeply ironic and symbolic tableau, as husband and wife bend over the coffin of his mistress and child. It is symbolic both of sexual compulsion and the power of social class, with their attendant patterns of betrayal.

Far from the Madding Crowd is an intensely visual novel. Its more striking scenes include the startling image of Gabriel Oak and Bathsheba Everdene perilously defying the cosmos on the rick in the storm, the lantern illuminating Troy's uniform when his spur is symbolically entangled with Bathsheba's skirt in the fir plantation, and Troy's performance as Dick Turpin at Greenhill Fair. As so often in Hardy's novels, such scenes involve an observer. Gabriel Oak watches Bathsheba through a hole in the hut where she is tending two cows with her aunt, while Troy observes Bathsheba talking with Boldwood through a slash in the tent at Greenhill Fair. As well as its visual effects, *Far from the Madding Crowd* displays

Hardy's narrative skills in his use of melodrama, ballad stories and psychological exploration. These are fused and held together by a detailed realism that relies not only upon descriptions of agricultural life, but on the evocation of a traditional community whose continuity Hardy cherishes.

From Geoffrey Harvey, *The Complete Critical Guide to Thomas Hardy* (New York: Routledge), 2003.

2. Narrative Technique

RALPH W. V. ELLIOTT

Far from the Madding Crowd tells a story, the story of Bathsheba Everdene and her three suitors, and whether a story appeals to us or not depends to a great extent on the way it is told. On a first reading of the book we are probably not aware of the several devices Hardy uses to make and keep us interested in the story; and this is as it should be, for we don't really want the mechanics of story-telling to obtrude any more than we want to hear all the noises the engine makes or watch all its parts moving when we are driving a car. On the other hand, as soon as our interest in the novel becomes a critical interest, we want to know what makes it work, what methods the writer uses to make his story interesting and his characters alive, and how he manages the words he uses.

Two important related aspects of Hardy's narrative technique are *continuity* and *the use of allusion*. We can consider continuity under three heads: rhythm, style and action. Right from the beginning of *Far from the Madding Crowd*, Hardy achieves a leisurely rhythm that sets the pace for the whole novel. I suggested earlier that this rhythm reflects the natural progress of country life with its regular recurrence of seasons and duties and festivities, and that Hardy skilfully weaves the important experiences of his characters into the natural cycle of rustic life. In this way we are carried naturally and smoothly from the opening of the story in the winter-month of December on to St Valentine's Day in February, into the spring, into the summer when Troy first appears and so on through the changing seasons. But this continuity is also one of style, of patterns and the movements of sentences which carry us steadily through the novel. This is easily illustrated from almost every page of the book, for example:

> When Farmer Oak smiled, the corners of his mouth spread till they were within an unimportant distance of his ears, his eyes were reduced to chinks, and diverging wrinkles appeared round them, extending upon his countenance like the rays in a rudimentary sketch of the rising sun. (ch.1)
>
> For a moment Boldwood stood so inertly after this that his soul seemed to have been entirely exhaled with the breath of his passionate words. He turned his face away, and withdrew, and his form was soon covered over the twilight as his footsteps mixed in with the low hiss of the leafy trees. (ch. 31)

Thirdly, the continuity is one of action. The story is never allowed to lag; it progresses steadily, rhythmically from one incident to the next. Hardy introduces his principal characters gradually, but once they have appeared on the stage of the novel we never lose sight of them for long. Even the chapters in which the rustic chorus gathers and discourses sometimes at considerable length are important links in the chain of events, and help to maintain that regular rhythm so characteristic of *Far from the Madding Crowd.* Variations in the tempo of the narrative do, of course, occur. A musical work is no less a unified composition for including fast and slow movements, and in the same way, a novel has episodes which move at different speeds. The opening scene of *Far from the Madding Crowd,* for instance, is extremely leisurely. Such words as 'exceedingly mild', 'perfectly still', 'sat motionless', 'idly' (repeated several times), 'reverie' express the leisurely movement as much as the even flow of the paragraphs and steady rhythm of the sentences. Troy's waiting in church (ch.16), punctuated by the ticking of the clock, is another good example of slow movement which will repay close study. On the other hand, there is the 'feverish' chapter 34 with its rapid dialogue of short, quick sentences, the whole racing towards its climax, as Boldwood discovers the marriage and Troy triumphantly locks himself into Bathsheba's house with 'another peal of laughter'. That such a tempo is the exception in *Far from the Madding Crowd* helps to underline the fact that the basic movement of the narrative, one of orderly progress, is what the musician would call *andante,* 'at a walking pace'. That this basic movement can span different periods of time in the action of the novel is apparent from a comparison, for example, of chapters 42 and 49: the former covers a few hours, from the collection of Fanny's coffin at the Casterbridge workhouse to its depositing in Bathsheba's sitting-room; the latter opens 'in the later autumn' and within a few pages moves on steadily, rhythmically, to 'the late summer' of the following year. Such is the unobtrusiveness of Hardy's narrative art.

This narrative continuity is helped along also by repeated allusions to what is to come. Our interest is sharpened, our appetite whetted, by such hints; they make us want to read on. Look at the following passages in their contexts and you will see how important their allusive function is in sustaining our interest:

> Luckily for the present, unluckily for her future tranquillity, her understanding had not yet told her what Boldwood was. (ch. 18)
>
> Subsequent events caused one of the verses to be remembered for many months, and even years, by more than one of those who were gathered there. (ch. 23)
>
> The impending night appeared to concentrate in his eye. (ch. 31)
>
> His mind sped into the future, and saw there enacted in years of leisure the scenes of repentance that would ensue from this work of haste. (ch. 35)
>
> 'Ring for some more brandy, Pennyways, I felt awful shudder just then!' (ch. 52)
>
> 'More harm may come of this than we know of.' (ch. 53)

Another method Hardy uses to sustain our interest is akin to *suspense,* although this is perhaps too strong a word for so unsensational a novel as *Far from the Madding Crowd.* Suspense, of course, means keying the reader up to a high pitch of excitement and expectancy, and then leaving him suspended, dangling, while the scene of action is temporarily shifted, as in the famous porter-scene in Shakespeare's *Macbeth.* There is, in Sections IV and VII (of chapter 52), a sharp contrast as we watch Troy drinking and smoking and laughing, preparing to reclaim Bathsheba, for she is after all good-looking and wealthy—and his wife. Yet the feeling of menace is here too: 'Ring for some more brandy, Pennyways, I felt an awful shudder just then!' Another good example of such interrupted narrative is the break at the end of ch. 16: Fanny has mistaken the church in which she was to have been married—a mistake of grave consequence to all the main actors in the novel—and Troy, 'with a light irony, and turning from her walked rapidly away.' At this tense moment, the scene shifts, we are left in suspense as to Fanny's fate and turn to Boldwood instead. We become absorbed in the progress of the latter's wooing of Bathsheba until she almost promises to be his wife—and then Troy reappears on the scene, and ch. 24 closes with the ominous remark, 'It was a fatal omission of Boldwood's that he had never once told her she was beautiful.'—a remark which we recall with some wistfulness when in ch. 53—far too late—Boldwood says to Bathsheba:

> 'You are still a very beautiful woman' . . . .
> However, it had not much effect now . . . .

Hardy makes use of suspense also in the tent-episode in ch. 50 and for a short time we are left in doubt regarding Boldwood's ultimate fate after his trial and sentence. Although suspense means interrupting the narrative, it is yet an agent of continuity, because it keeps our interest alive and makes us want to read on.

Dialogue is an instrument both of characterization and of narrative in a novel. Characters reveal themselves as they speak, and events can be created, reported, or discussed in conversation. If you read *Far from the Madding Crowd* carefully, you will notice the many different uses to which dialogue is put, and you will see how Hardy handles it, often convincingly, sometimes not very successfully. A good example of the importance of dialogue is to be found in the first two meetings between Bathsheba and Troy. Troy is an accomplished talker; and the mixture of charm, flattery, and persuasive flow of language (his 'rare invention' Bathsheba calls it in ch. 26) overwhelms her:

> Bathsheba really knew not what to say. (ch. 24)
> Bathsheba was absolutely speechless. (ch. 26)

and she capitulates with one final, unfinished, helpless stammer:

> 'No—that is—I certainly have heard Liddy say they do, but—' . . . .
> Never did a fragile tailless sentence convey a more perfect meaning.
> (ch. 26)

Not all the dialogue in these two chapters is handled with equal skill, however. Towards the end of ch. 26 the conversation between Troy and Bathsheba becomes stilted, and has an unnatural ring about it which detracts from its effectiveness. The same is sometimes true of the speech of the rustic characters. Matthew Moon, as we know him from ch. 10, is hardly likely to have spoken like this:

> ''Twas only wildness that made him a soldier, and maids rather like your man of sin.' (ch. 33)

Nor would words like these have come naturally to William Smallbury or any other of the rustic chorus for that matter:

> 'Every looker-on's inside shook with the blows of the great drum to his deepest vitals.' (ch. 10)

That Hardy came to be aware of such lapses, perhaps as a result of contemporary criticism, is suggested by occasional changes introduced into the novel when, after initial publication as a serial in 1874, it was reprinted in book form. Thus, for example, the world 'philandering' was changed to the much more likely, and picturesque, colloquialism 'smack-and-coddle' in Gabriel's 'none of that dalliance-talk—that smack-and-coddle style of yours—about Miss Everdene' in ch. 15.

But such instances are greatly outnumbered by Hardy's effective and convincing passages of dialogue. Most of the rustic speech rings true, with its double negatives and wrong pronouns and generous sprinkling of dialect words:

> 'Our mis'ess has too much sense under they knots of black hair to do such a mad thing.' (ch. 33)

> 'She won't be in Bath by no daylight!' (ch. 32)
> 'And you whop and slap at your work without any trouble, and everything goes on like sticks a-breaking.' (ch.42)

In the same way the speech of the main actors reflects their natures and remains true to character: Oak's slow, measured speech ('I can't match you, I know, in mapping out my mind upon my tongue', ch. 3) reflects his temperament as convincingly as Troy's banter and 'rare invention' reflect his. And as the characters react to different situations or change, like Boldwood and Bathsheba, in the course of the novel, so does their speech vary or alter while yet remaining true to character. We would not expect Boldwood to talk at the end of the novel, when jealousy and shattered hopes have driven him to the verge of madness, as he had done at the beginning. To gauge the difference we need only compare the 'deep voice' of Boldwood's first words in ch. 9 with 'the thin tones' which 'hardly a soul in the assembly recognized . . . to be those of Boldwood in ch. 53, and to examine like milestones along this road the solemn offer of marriage to Bathsheba in ch. 19, the frenzied utterances to Troy in ch. 34, the curt responses to Oak in ch. 38, and the feverish search for reassurance in ch. 52.

In all the Wessex novels Hardy relies to a great extent on description and the creation of atmosphere as aids to narrative. The rustic environment, as we have seen, is of great importance in *Far from the Madding Crowd*, hence the rustic chorus, the rustic dialogue, and the use of the natural environment as almost a live character. The scenes where important incidents occur are closely and accurately described and made memorable for us by a skilful selection of detail. Detail, often minute, is indeed the key to Hardy's descriptive technique, whether it is of a face, a building, a landscape, or a storm. Oak's watch in ch. 1, Bathsheba's house in ch. 9, the pool and meadow in ch. 19, the fog in ch. 42 – these are just a few examples of longer descriptions which will repay careful study. Bathsheba's house, to take one of these examples, gave Hardy the opportunity to make use of the architectural knowledge which he had acquired during his apprenticeship and employment as an architect in his early manhood. It is an old house, as Hardy reminds us several times in the novel ('a hoary building', ch.9; 'the mouldy pile', ch. 13; 'Bathsheba's crannied and mouldy halls', ch.

32), once a manorial hall whose pillared front now has a sleepy look, and whose columnar chimneys and coped gables remain as witnesses of past grandeur. There are mosses on the stone tiling and along the front path. It is at the back of the building, facing the courtyard of farm buildings, that its present animation resides. The inside has as much the aura of age as the outside, with its heavy oak staircase, balusters, and railing, its warped and creaking floors, and rattling doors and windows. No wonder that 'the atmosphere of the place seemed as old as the walls' (ch. 13) and that it was a cold and cheerless 'bower' in winter.

But descriptions need not be long to be effective. A vista or a facial expression can be caught, as by a camera, in one poignant phrase:

> Hennery shook his head, and smiled one of the bitter smiles, dragging all the flesh of his forehead into a corrugated heap in the centre. (ch. 15)
>
> He lingered and lingered on, till there was no difference between the eastern and western expanses of sky, and the timid hares began to limp courageously round the dim hillocks (ch. 34)

The corrugated heap, the limping hares are as much an indication of Hardy's accuracy of observation and knowledge and use of detail as the list of flowers for Fanny's hearse (ch. 41), or the breeds of sheep at the Greenhill Fair (ch. 50). These details add authenticity as well as atmosphere to the novel, for atmosphere is not merely the writing of ornamental 'purple' passages, largely for their own sakes, but rather the creation of a setting or of the mood of a scene in which the reader can believe either because of its realistic or because of its imaginative truth. Perhaps it is just because the descriptive details chosen are often so minute and intimate, that we believe all the more readily in the truth of the scene and enter into its mood. You will find numerous examples in the novel of such convincing detail; consider, for instance, how Oak puts out his light in ch. 2: he does not merely extinguish it, but 'extinguished the lantern by blowing into it and then pinching the snuff'. Just what is the force of these additional details? Or analyse for yourselves the effect of this piece of close observation at the beginning of ch. 35:

> The creeping plants about the old manor-house were bowed with rows of heavy water drops, which had upon objects behind them the effect of minute lenses of high magnifying power.

Such passages are doubtlessly 'ornamental,' but that is rarely their only function. You will remember Professor Bonamy Dobree's view, quoted earlier, that Hardy's descriptions 'are never mere decoration,' because the natural world plays such an important role in Hardy's novels. If the natural world is considered to be alive and active, then the function of descriptions of scenes and seasons is to relate the natural world closely to the activities of the human actors in whom we are interested. The harmony established between natural setting and human mood, previously mentioned, depends upon descriptive detail that will create the appropriate atmosphere. Again, this can be done as effectively in a sentence as in a paragraph; in either way Hardy excels, and often it is the poet in him who speaks.

When Boldwood goes to confront Bathsheba after the valentine incident, 'the ground was melodious with ripples, and the sky with larks' (ch. 18). When the great storm approaches, Oak's apprehensions are reflected not merely by the 'sinister aspect' of the night, but by the instinctive actions of various animals; each actor, natural, human, animal, conveys the atmosphere of impending terrors (ch. 36). In ch. 43, Bathsheba, restless and racked by suspicions and uncertainty, leaves her house to seek advice from Oak and immediately enters Oak's serene world, where 'every blade, every twig was still. The air was yet thick with moisture, though somewhat less dense than during the afternoon, and a steady smack of drops upon the fallen leaves under the boughs was almost musical in its soothing regularity.' The 'soothing regularity' outside is the image of the peaceful scene inside Gabriel's cottage, where he is seen first reading, then praying, and it is what Bathsheba seeks but cannot find. The contrast between her world and his, her 'wretchedness in full activity' and 'the atmosphere of content which seemed to spread from that little dwelling' is underlined by the fact that the natural world is sharing Oak's serenity. Bathsheba is isolated and becomes even more so as she returns home, her mission unfulfilled, 'soothing regularity' left far behind. And so the chapter moves on to its tremendous, terrifying climax.

Now and again a touch of humour enters into one of Hardy's descriptions, as when he is speaking of the Casterbridge workhouse, relieving for a moment the tension of ch. 40, but humour in *Far from the Madding Crowd* belongs mainly to the rustics. Collectively as well as individually the country people are made to convey the impression that there is a good deal of comedy in life to compensate for its hardships. In the later Wessex novels, this impression markedly decreases, but in *Far from the Madding Crowd* the rustic interludes are largely comic ones. From the beginning we are made aware that the Weatherbury folk 'were as hardy, merry, thriving, wicked a set as any in the whole country' (ch. 6), and the rest of the novel bears this out. Chs. 8 and 15 in the malthouse, ch. 10 in the old hall, ch. 42 in the Buck's Head deserve close study in this connection. What does their humorous content contribute to the novel as a whole? Is it mere light relief? Or is it a more serious comment on human life and affairs? Nor should we forget, when seeking answers to these questions, that the chapters just mentioned are in every case contrasted with chapters in which Fanny Robin appears: in ch. 7 Oak meets Fanny by the churchyard wall, in ch. 11 Fanny visits Troy's barracks, in ch. 16 she was to have married Troy, and ch. 42 is dominated by her coffin. Fanny is as much a member of the country community as the others, but throughout the novel she stands apart. The contrast between Fanny's tragedy and the comic chorus is an important ingredient of *Far from the Madding Crowd,* perhaps nowhere more obviously so than in ch. 42. The choice of Joseph Poorgrass, who would tremble and blush with terror at the slightest provocation (*see* ch. 15), as the driver Fanny's hearse is in itself a stroke of genius. No wonder that 'his spirits were oozing out of him quite' as he finds himself and his peculiar burden enveloped in a fog with its 'unfathomable gloom amid the high trees on each hand, indistinct, shadowless, and spectre-like in their monochrome of grey'. To say that 'he felt anything but cheerful' is a delightful understatement. And then comes the crowing moment of comedy as Joseph joins Coggan and Clark in the Buck's Head to drink himself into a state of blissful forgetfulness while the body of poor Fanny lies outside on its waggon under the trees.

Among the most entertaining passages in the rustic interludes are undoubtedly those in which we get glimpse of such outsiders as Coggan's first wife Charlotte or Bathsheba's parents. The charge of coarseness which contemporary reviewers levelled against Hardy for his inclusion of the story of Bathsheba's father in ch. 8 is one to which modern readers of the novel would probably not subscribe. The present generation, nurtured on stronger meat, is not likely to wince at the humorous account of a husband, 'faithful and true enough' to his marriage-vow, but with a roving eye, asking his wife to take off her wedding-ring in order to fancy her still only his sweetheart, so that 'as soon as he could thoroughly fancy he was doing wrong and committing the seventh, 'a got to like her as well as ever, and they lived on a perfect picture of a mutel love.'

The fact that, as Poorgrass points out, 'a happy Providence kept it from being any worse. You see, he might have gone the bad road and given his eyes to unlawfulness entirely—yes, gross unlawfulness, so to say it,' and that Mr Everdene became in his old age a right godly man who 'took to saying "Amen" almost as loud as the clerk,' did not prevent Hardy from laying himself open to the charge of coarseness in Victorian England. Why then the inclusion of such material in *Far from the Madding Crowd?* How far is it relevant to the story, to the development of character, to atmosphere? Atmosphere is certainly created, or enhanced, by these homely details gossiped about in Warren's Malthouse, and much of the rustic wit and shrewdness is expended on just these topics. Whether Hardy intended the reader to draw any conclusions about Bathsheba herself from the fickleness and marital oddities of her father, we can only surmise. In several of the Wessex novels fathers and mothers play not inconsiderable parts, so perhaps this comic glimpse of Bathsheba's father is not quite as irrelevant as might at first appear.

Elsewhere in the novel, humour is largely incidental and almost wholly verbal. It consists mainly of witty comments or comparisons and occasionally takes the form of irony.

From Ralph W.V. Elliott, *Far from the Madding Crowd*
(London: Macmillan Critical Commentaries), 1966.

TOPICS FOR DISCUSSION

1. Illustrate the changes that Bathsheba's character displays in the course of the novel. Discuss the nature of these changes and how they affect the plot.
2. Attempt a character study of Gabriel Oak.
3. Compare and contrast the three suitors of Bathsheba. What is their influence on her?
4. Consider the roles of Fanny Robin and Liddy Smallbury in the novel.
5. Discuss the title '*Far from the Madding Crowd.*'
6. What part do the rustic and minor characters play in the novel?
7. Discuss
   a. the Wessex landscape and its effect on the action
   b. rustic humour
   c. Hardy's descriptive style.
8. Which scene in the novel did you like best of all? Why?
9. How does Troy impress Bathsheba before her marriage? What are her feelings after her marriage?
10. How does Hardy use fate and coincidence in this novel?
11. Assess and analyse the character of Boldwood. How does he become a tragic character?
12. The marriage of Gabriel Oak and Bathsheba is the climax of the events in the story. Discuss.

FURTHER READING

Primary Sources

The Return of the Native (1878)
The Trumpet Major (1880)
The Mayor of Casterbridge (1886)
The Woodlanders (1887)
Wessex Tales (1888)
Tess of the D'Urbervilles (1891)
Jude the Obscure (1896)
Wessex Poems (1898)

Secondary Sources

Bayley-John. *An Essay on Hardy*. Cambridge: Cambridge University Press, 1978.

Cecil, Lord David. *Hardy the Novelist: An Essay in Criticism.* London: Constable, 1943.

Draper, R. P. ed. *Thomas Hardy: Three Pastoral Novels: A Casebook.* London: Macmillan, 1987.

Elliott, Ralph W. V. *Hardy: Far from the Madding Crowd.* London: Macmillan, 1966.

Harvey, Geoffrey. *The Complete Critical Guide to Thomas Hardy.* New York: Routledge, 2003.

Kramer, Dale. *The Cambridge Companion to Thomas Hardy.* Cambridge: Cambridge University Press, 1999.

Langbaum, Robert. *Thomas Hardy in our Time.* Basingstoke: Macmillan, 1995.

Peck, John. *How to Study a Thomas Hardy Novel.* London: Macmillan, 1987.